The

THE GOLDEN GLOBE

Anakin and his new friend Tahiri take a forbidden trip down a river near the Jedi academy. They are drawn by the Force—but for all they know it could be the dark side!

LYRIC'S WORLD

Anakin and Tahiri discover carvings deep within the caves of Yavin 8. These carvings might be able to break the curse of the Golden Globe! But there is something waiting for them in the caves . . .

PROMISES

Before she joined the academy, Tahiri lived with the strange and dangerous Sand People of Tatooine. To learn about her real parents, she and Anakin will have to use the Force like never before . . .

ANAKIN'S QUEST

Anakin has been having terrible dreams of a secret cave on Dagobah. What is inside? And will Anakin be strong enough in the Force to face it?

Don't miss the thrilling
Junior Jedi adventure . . .
KENOBI'S BLADE

STAR WARS®
Junior Jedi Knights
Vader's Fortress

Rebecca Moesta

BERKLEY JAM BOOKS, NEW YORK

To my parents,
Louis and Louise Moesta.
I love you.

STAR WARS: JUNIOR JEDI KNIGHTS: VADER'S FORTRESS

A Berkley Jam Book / published by arrangement with
Lucasfilm Ltd.

PRINTING HISTORY
Boulevard edition / July 1997
Berkley Jam edition / January 1999

All rights reserved.
®, ™ & copyright © 1997 by Lucasfilm Ltd.
Cover illustration by Eric Lee.
Material excerpted from KENOBI'S BLADE © 1997 by Lucasfilm Ltd.
This book may not be reproduced in whole or in part,
by mimeograph or any other means, without permission.
For information address: The Berkley Publishing Group,
a division of Penguin Putnam Inc.,
375 Hudson Street, New York, New York 10014.

The Penguin Putnam Inc. World Wide Web site address is
http://www.penguinputnam.com

Make sure to check out *PB Plug*,
the science fiction/fantasy newsletter, at
http://www.pbplug.com

ISBN: 0-425-16956-1

BERKLEY JAM BOOKS®
Berkley Jam Books are published by The Berkley Publishing Group,
a division of Penguin Putnam Inc.,
375 Hudson Street, New York, New York 10014.
BERKLEY JAM and its logo are trademarks
belonging to Penguin Putnam Inc.

PRINTED IN THE UNITED STATES OF AMERICA

10 9 8 7 6 5 4

ACKNOWLEDGMENTS

Thanks to Lillie E. Mitchell and her tireless enthusiasm in transcribing my dictation; Katie Tyree, Catherin Ulatowski, and Angela Kato at WordFire, Inc., for their help in keeping the work flowing; Lucy Wilson of Lucasfilm for having faith in me, and Sue Rostoni of Lucasfilm for her many helpful suggestions; Steve Sansweet and Allan Kausch at Lucasfilm for their encouragement; Bill Smith and West End Games for their wonderful resource materials; Dave Dorman and Eric Lee for their inspired artwork; Richard Curtis for his assistance in my writing career; Ginjer Buchanan at Berkley for her wholehearted support and patience; Jonathan MacGregor Cowan for being my enthusiastic assistant and test reader; and Kevin J. Anderson, as always, for being my cheerleader, coach, and inspiration.

A heartfelt thanks to the following people for paving the way and for many useful discussions:

Kevin J. Anderson
Nancy Richardson
Roger MacBride Allen
A. C. Crispin
Barbara Hambly
Michael P. Kube-McDowell
Vonda McIntyre
Steve Perry
Kristine Kathryn Rusch
Michael A. Stackpole
Kathy Tyers
Dave Wolverton
Timothy Zahn

ONE

Drops of moisture sparkled on the short grass of the landing field in front of the Jedi academy. The sunlight on Yavin 4 seemed especially bright after the morning's rain. Smells of leaves and flowers drifted from the jungle nearby. The air felt comfortably damp and warm to Anakin Solo, who gazed expectantly toward the sky. He brushed his fringe of straight brown bangs away from his ice blue eyes and then shaded them with one hand so that he could see better.

The ship should arrive soon, he thought.

Anakin's best friend Tahiri stood beside him, barefoot on the grassy stubble. Her pale yellow hair blew free in the breeze, and her sea green eyes also looked skyward. Beside her waited

1

Uldir, the strong teenage son of two cargo pilots. Shaggy chestnut hair framed his proud face. Uldir had stowed away and come to the Jedi academy in hopes of becoming a Jedi. He had persuaded Anakin's uncle, Luke Skywalker, to accept him as a Jedi trainee for a while, even though the teen had no real talent with the Force. Although Uldir was several years older than Anakin, the two youngest Jedi trainees had befriended the new student.

Both Tahiri and Uldir were unusually silent today, and Anakin felt himself growing impatient. "We've been waiting almost an hour," Anakin said. "Do you think something's wrong?"

Uldir shrugged. Tahiri didn't respond. Anakin shifted his weight. So far, he had managed to amuse himself by solving puzzles in his head, but he was getting tired of standing. He wanted to sit down, but he knew the wet grass would soak his comfortable flightsuit in no time. He wasn't sure that would feel any better than just standing.

Even though Tahiri was a couple of years younger than he was, the long wait this morning didn't seem to bother her at all. Uldir whistled a tune under his breath and retied the belt of his new brown Jedi robe. Anakin guessed it made Uldir feel more like a student to have a robe like the ones Jedi Masters often wore.

A Jedi needs to be patient, Anakin reminded

himself. Taking a deep breath, he did one of his calming exercises using the Force. He thought back on the quest that had recently taken them all to the planet Dagobah. He, Tahiri, and Uldir had had many adventures there, guided by the Jedi Master Ikrit. One at a time, the three junior Jedi had gone into a special cave to find out about who they were inside themselves. In the cave Anakin and Tahiri had learned that their parents and the people in their past were a part of who each of them was today. But they also learned that only their *own* choices could decide whom they would become now. Uldir had seen nothing in the cave, though, and Anakin wondered if the older boy had learned anything.

"I don't think so," Tahiri said suddenly. Just like that, with no explanation.

"Huh?" Anakin blinked at her. "*What* don't you think?"

Tahiri shrugged. "I don't think that there's anything wrong, of course. That *is* what you asked, isn't it? You asked if I thought that anything was wrong. And I don't. So I said—"

"Yes . . . yes, I heard you," Anakin said. "I only meant—"

Tahiri gave him an odd look. "Really, Anakin! Sometimes I wonder how you manage to get so confused even during a simple conversation. And anyway, I don't know why you'd think that anything might be wrong. Master Skywalker wouldn't have sent us out here to meet Tionne if he hadn't been sure she was going to arrive sooner or later. So I'm positive that everything is fine. Relax and enjoy the beautiful weather. She'll be here any time now."

"Well, I hope she hurries," Uldir said. His amber eyes searched the sky. "I don't have much time before my next shift working in the kitchen. I thought we were going to go into the jungle together so you could give me some tips on using the Force to lift leaves."

"We'll have plenty of time to practice," Tahiri said confidently.

"I just wish there was an easier way to learn about the Force," Uldir said. His voice had started low, but changed with a squeak in midsentence. "It always seems like such hard work."

"I guess I don't think about whether it's hard to study the Force and practice, because I enjoy it so much," Anakin admitted.

Tahiri gave Uldir an encouraging smile. "I have a feeling you're going to start catching on pretty soon now. After all, when Tionne found me on Tatooine—"

"That's Uncle Luke's homeworld, you know," Anakin explained to Uldir.

"Right," Tahiri said. "Anyway, when Tionne found me out in the middle of the desert living with the Sand People, I didn't know any more about using the Force than you—but look how much I've learned already. Tionne is a natural teacher, and I'm never bored when she's talking. That's why I love to go along on her research trips, you know. I wish I could have gone with her this time to Borgo Prime. . . . I always learn so much." Tahiri looked pensive for a moment; then her face brightened. "Well, she did promise to take me along on her next research trip. Traveling with her is always an adventure. I hope—"

"That sounds fun," Anakin said. "I wonder if she'd mind if I came along with you."

"Yeah, me too," Uldir said.

"Well, you can ask her yourself," Tahiri said, pointing upward. "That must be her now. But where did she get that strange ship? I've never seen it before."

A ship had indeed arrived and was floating down through the air toward the landing field. The craft was very old and had a strange design, with a plump reddish-orange body and broad solar sails that collected sunlight to power the ship. The shimmering metallic sails spread out on each side like wings, making the craft look something like a pudgy copper dragon.

Tahiri seemed to dance with excitement as they waited for the ship to land. When the orange sails finally folded and the spacecraft touched down, Tahiri could contain herself no longer. She ran forward, shouting a greeting as her good friend and Jedi instructor Tionne stepped down from the odd little ship.

Anakin wanted to give the two of them a chance to talk before he joined them, so he hung back for a moment with Uldir. He could sense through the Force that Tionne was just as giddy as the blonde-haired girl, but he couldn't tell what the excitement was about.

Watching the talkative girl and the quiet Jedi instructor together always made Anakin smile. In spite of their differences, the two shared a close bond. They could almost be mother and daughter, Anakin mused. Since Tahiri's mother had died when she was only three, he wondered if she did think of the Jedi teacher that way.

Beside Anakin, Uldir cleared his throat impatiently and fidgeted with his robe. "Okay," Anakin said, "I guess we can go help Tionne now." They started forward.

"Welcome back," Anakin called.

"Hi," Uldir said.

Tionne turned. Her large mother-of-pearl eyes sparkled with delight at seeing them. "It's good to be back," she said. "Even better because I have such exciting news for Master Skywalker."

"So you found something?" Anakin asked.

Tionne smiled in an I've-got-a-secret kind of way. "Quite a bit, actually. But first, what do you think of my new ship?"

Uldir snorted. "If that's a *new* model, then I'm the son of a nerf herder."

The silvery-haired instructor gave a musical laugh. "You're right, of course. The *Lore Seeker*—that's what I named my ship—is really quite old. That's why I loved the design so much."

"Well, I think the ship is perfect for you," Tahiri said. "It's just right. And so is the name."

Anakin nodded. He knew Tionne had called her craft the *Lore Seeker* because she loved to look for stories and legends about Jedi who lived long ago. He closed his eyes for a moment and reached into the ship with his mind then looked up at Tionne with surprise. "It's in excellent condition," he announced.

"I'm glad to hear you say that," the Jedi instructor said with a smile. "I thought so, too. But because the ship was so old, I was able to buy it from a Randoni trader for a song."

"How much did you *really* pay?" Uldir asked.

Tionne shrugged. "Just a song. Really. While I was looking for Jedi legends, I came across an ancient song that told about the very first Randoni merchants and the vaults where they hid their wealth. The trader was so interested that she offered me the *Lore Seeker* in exchange for the song. Now come help me unload my cargo, and I'll show you some of my other treasures."

Anakin and Tahiri needed no more urging. They hurried to explore the strange ship and help Tionne. Uldir grumbled something about never getting the fun jobs, but he went along with them anyway.

Inside the *Lore Seeker*'s tiny hold, Tionne said, "You may carry this Twi'lek story-chain, Tahiri—each link tells a different part of a story. Please be very careful with it. Uldir, here is a holodisk. It holds a recording of some very old Jedi songs. Anakin, would you please carry this scroll? I'll take the tapestry."

On the way back to the Jedi academy they each carried their packages with extra care. As usual, Tahiri chattered gaily. "I can't wait to see Master Skywalker's face when you show him everything you found. He'll probably want to see the *Lore Seeker* right away. Have you learned any of the old songs from that holodisk yet? Will you sing them to us?"

"You sure seem to have had a successful trip," Anakin put in.

Tionne tossed back her silvery hair and chuckled. "Oh, that's not all—I found something even more important. I learned where to find an object that may have more meaning for Master Skywalker than any of these treasures we're holding."

"Well, where is it then?" Tahiri said.

"In an old fortress on a planet called Vjun," Tionne said.

"Does anyone live in the fortress?" Anakin asked.

Tionne shook her head. "Not anymore."

"Well, if it's really that important, don't you think you ought to go find it?" Tahiri said. "And don't forget that you promised to take me with you this time."

"I'd like to go along, too," Anakin added.

"Yeah, it sounds like fun," Uldir said.

Tionne frowned. "I'm not sure Master Skywalker will approve. It could be a bit dangerous. The news about this special thing had just reached Borgo Prime, but there might be other people who learned about where it is—other people who might want to find it too."

"Then it sounds important enough that we ought to go after it," Tahiri insisted. "As soon as possible."

"Why would someone else want it?" Anakin asked, his ice blue eyes alive with curiosity. "What kind of special object is this?"

Tionne's face lit with a wondering smile, and she gave a happy sigh. "It's Obi-Wan Kenobi's lightsaber!"

TWO

Luke Skywalker, dressed in a comfortable black flightsuit, sat on the stone floor in the room where he meditated and did his office work. At the moment, though, Luke was not meditating.

Before him in the center of the room stood his barrel-shaped blue and white droid, Artoo-Detoo. It was time for Artoo's routine cleaning.

Anakin's older sister Jaina often helped Luke with this chore, but the Jedi Master didn't mind doing it himself. He actually found it relaxing. With his tools neatly laid out on the floor and fresh packets of lubricant beside him, Master Skywalker opened Artoo-Detoo's front panels and got to work. After checking the droid's numerous electrical connections, Luke added a few gadgets and upgrades Jaina had scrounged up for Artoo: a retractable mirror attachment, a power booster for the comm unit, and a new focusing lens for the hologram projector.

A white-furred creature with floppy ears watched from his favorite perch on top of Artoo-Detoo's domed head. Most people at the Jedi academy thought the quiet, friendly creature was Anakin's pet, but Ikrit was really a Jedi Master himself.

Luke had just begun to drain dirty, oily grunge from the droid's wheel axles when he heard a knock on the heavy wooden door.

"Would you get that, please?" Luke asked Ikrit. The fluffy-furred Jedi Master sprang down from the top of Artoo's head and bounded toward the arched doorway. Then he reached up, unhooked the latch, and opened the door.

Luke looked up from the packet of slippery lubricant he held in his hand, then smiled when he saw who his visitors were. "Come in," he said, "all of you."

His words seemed to open an invisible dam, because people and noises instantly flooded into his quiet room. Luke laughed as everyone tried to talk to him at once.

"Master Skywalker, I have wonderful news," Tionne said.

"You'll never guess in a million years," Tahiri added.

"Can I go with them?" Anakin asked.

"Yeah, me too!" Uldir said. "I don't want to get left behind."

Luke put down the lubricant and chuckled. "All right, I'm ready to hear your news," he said as Artoo-Detoo warbled enthusiastically. "Let's start with Tionne."

Luke was amazed. He thought back to the last time he had seen Obi-Wan Kenobi's lightsaber. Kenobi, Luke's first Jedi instructor, had fought Darth Vader on the first Death Star. The old man had sacrificed himself so that Luke, the Wookiee Chewbacca, and Anakin's parents Han and Leia could escape in the *Millennium Falcon*.

"Let me get this straight," Luke said. "Someone on Borgo Prime—an information broker— told you that Obi-Wan Kenobi's lightsaber was taken away from the Death Star before it blew up?"

"That's right," Tionne said. "The Hutt who sold me the information said that the lightsaber was taken to the planet Vjun and hidden in some sort of fortress or castle. But it's all right—no one lives there anymore."

"Darth Vader . . . ," Luke said. It surprised him that Darth Vader would want to keep the lightsaber of his former teacher, but it wasn't impossible. Vader could have sent it away from the Death Star just after he defeated Kenobi. Or he might even have taken it with him when he escaped the destruction of the Death Star.

"What *about* Darth Vader?" Tionne asked in confusion.

"That fortress," Luke answered. He pulled some wires from a panel inside Artoo-Detoo, cleaned the contacts, and reattached the wires. "I've been there. It's called Bast Castle, and it belonged to my father when he was known as Darth Vader."

Luke heard Anakin draw in a sharp breath. Tahiri gasped and looked at Anakin. Uldir gave a low whistle.

"Maybe that explains why the broker on Borgo Prime said that only 'the family' had a right to claim the lightsaber," Tionne said. "I thought he was talking about Obi-Wan's family, but maybe he meant *you*. Luke, we have to hurry. This is brand-new information, but if *I* found out about it, someone else could too. I'd like your permission to go to Vjun and look for Kenobi's lightsaber. You could come with me if you like."

Luke thought for a moment and gave a small shake of his head. "I'm afraid I can't. The Chief of State—my sister Leia—has called me back for an urgent meeting on Coruscant."

"If Mom needs you on Coruscant, then Tahiri and I would like to go with Tionne," Anakin said in a serious voice. "Please, Uncle Luke—it's important to me. I'm a member of the family, and I'd like to see this place where . . . where my grandfather lived."

Luke glanced at Ikrit, who sat atop the curve of Artoo-Detoo's head. The furry Jedi Master nodded. The planet Vjun would probably be deserted, Luke decided, and he trusted Tionne and the Jedi Master Ikrit to take good care of Anakin and Tahiri. Between the two Jedi— although Tionne did not yet know about Master Ikrit's true identity—they could handle almost any emergency that came up. Ikrit had certainly been a reliable teacher and guide when the junior Jedi had gone to Dagobah. Luke knew that the two children could continue their training in the Force as easily on the trip as they could here on Yavin 4. Two children, two Jedi. The experience would be excellent for Anakin and Tahiri, Luke concluded.

"Master Skywalker, I want to go wherever Anakin and Tahiri are going," Uldir said. His voice cracked as he spoke. "I'll probably learn more with them than if I just stayed here anyway."

Luke frowned and thought this over.

"Please say yes, Master Skywalker. You know he'd manage to come along somehow," Tionne said with a twinkle in her eye, "and the cargo hold in the *Lore Seeker* is much too small to carry our supplies *and* a stowaway."

Artoo gave one beep that meant yes in the

simple code that the droid and Anakin had developed.

Luke chuckled again. He knew of few better teachers than Tionne, and if she thought she could help this troubled teenager, perhaps it was best to let Uldir go along. "Very well," Luke said, coming to a decision. "But I'll have to arrange it with Uldir's parents first, and with Anakin's."

The junior Jedi cheered.

"*If* your parents say yes, then you can all go," Luke said. "But only on one condition."

Tionne nodded. "Of course."

"Sure," Tahiri said.

"Anything," Anakin added.

"What is it?" Uldir asked warily.

"Even though you won't be gone very long, I want you to take Ikrit and Artoo along with you, just as a precaution."

"Ikrit?" Tionne looked surprised. "Well, why not? I'm sure the children will enjoy having him along." Her face broke into a bright smile. "Oh, thank you, Master Skywalker," she said with obvious delight. "It's all settled then."

Luke thought about Ikrit and all the lore and legends that the old Jedi Master knew. "I hope you all learn a lot from this trip," he said. "Especially you, Tionne. You may be pleasantly surprised." Luke closed the front panel on Artoo-Detoo and wiped away the last traces of lubricant with a clean soft cloth. "There," he said. "Now Artoo-Detoo's all ready to go with you."

THREE

Tahiri usually sat beside her silvery-haired teacher when they went on research trips together, but because Artoo-Detoo was actually a copilot he sat next to Tionne instead today. Tahiri didn't mind, though. She gave a happy sigh and wriggled her bare toes. It felt good just to be traveling with Tionne again. And, with Ikrit settled on Artoo-Detoo's domed head, and Anakin and Uldir by her side in Tionne's new ship, Tahiri felt that this was turning out to be a true adventure.

Tionne seemed happy, too. She hummed as she entered their course into the navigation computer in front of her. "All right, Artoo,"

Tionne said, "we're ready to jump to hyperspace."

"I always love this part," Tahiri whispered to Anakin and Uldir as the little droid switched on the hyperdrive.

Uldir shrugged and said, "I've seen it a million times with my parents. I've flown a lot."

But Anakin leaned over and whispered to Tahiri, "I know what you mean. It's beautiful."

Tahiri sat back and watched the front viewports. In the blackness around them, swarms of sparkling stars stretched into glowing streaks as the *Lore Seeker* shot into hyperspace.

Artoo-Detoo twittered and bleeped proudly.

"Thank you, Artoo," Tionne said. "I could get used to having an experienced droid like you around."

The barrel-shaped droid made an embarrassed-sounding noise.

Tahiri giggled. "Maybe you'll have to train me instead, Tionne."

The instructor turned and grinned back at her. "I probably will. After all, Master Skywalker taught *me* a lot about flying."

"My dad says Uncle Luke was a pretty hot fighter pilot before he became a Jedi," Anakin said.

For a moment Uldir looked very interested, but then he snorted and said, "Any idiot can become a pilot—but being a Jedi is something special."

Tionne swiveled her seat around to look at the three junior Jedi. Her wide mother-of-pearl eyes were serious. "What's *really* special," she said in a stern voice, "is finding the things that you're good at, things that you enjoy, and then practicing until you become the best that you can be."

"Uh-oh. I think that's her way of telling us it's time for a lesson," Tahiri said.

The Jedi teacher smiled ruefully. "Yes, I suppose it is. We'll be in hyperspace for quite a while now. Artoo can let us know when we get closer to Vjun, so this would be a good time for me to do a bit of teaching. Let's see," she murmured. "What would be the best subject to teach about today?"

"How about lightsabers?" Anakin asked hopefully.

"Yeah, tell us about lightsabers," Uldir chimed in.

"I'd like that," Tahiri said.

"It *is* appropriate, isn't it?" Anakin asked. "Because of our quest."

"All right then." Tionne chuckled. "Lightsabers it is." She cleared her throat and began to speak in the musical voice she used whenever she taught. "For thousands of years, Jedi have used energy swords called lightsabers as their special weapons. Anyone can pick up a lightsaber and turn it on, but only someone trained in the Force can really use it well. The energy blades are powerful enough to slice through doors, helmets, people. . . . These weapons can be very dangerous to anyone who doesn't know how to use them.

"And so," Tionne concluded, "a Jedi Master waits until a student is mature enough and has enough skills in the Force before beginning lightsaber training."

"But how does a new Jedi student *get* a lightsaber in the first place?" Uldir asked.

Tahiri was glad that Uldir was so interested in what Tionne had to say, even though she knew he would probably have to train for many years before he could ever expect to have a lightsaber.

"Well, there are several ways that I know of," the instructor answered in her musical voice. "Most of the time a Jedi will spend weeks or even months choosing just the right parts for a lightsaber. For mine, I searched almost a year to find a spiral mist-horn to make the handle and the perfect crystal-pearl to use for the laser gem.

"When a Jedi builds a lightsaber, unless it is lost or destroyed the Jedi keeps it until death. Sometimes, though, a master or a parent who is a Jedi makes a gift of a lightsaber. In some cases, although it is rare," Tionne continued, "an old lightsaber may be discovered or a new one may be captured."

"Uncle Luke said that his first lightsaber once belonged to his father before he became Darth Vader," Anakin said.

"That's right," Tionne said. "But after he lost his hand and his lightsaber at Cloud City, Luke was forced to build a new one."

Uldir nodded thoughtfully. "So Master Skywalker inherited the first one and built his next one. . . . Do all Jedi carry lightsabers, then?"

Tahiri was amazed that Uldir still found the subject so fascinating.

Tionne's huge pearly eyes grew unfocused, as if she were trying to remember something. "In the past there were some Jedi who did not carry lightsabers—at least not all the time," she said. "There is a legend about a Jedi named Nomi Sunrider. She refused to touch a lightsaber for a long time after using one against her husband's murderers. She didn't fight with a lightsaber again until she had to save her daughter and her Jedi Master. But the lightsaber is more than just a weapon. It is a *symbol* of the Jedi. Nowadays I think that all Jedi, once they are fully trained, carry their lightsabers with—"

"No. Not all Jedi." Ikrit, who had been completely silent up until now, spoke from where he sat on Artoo-Detoo's head.

Tionne blinked in surprise. "Anakin, does

your pet know what he just said?" Tahiri saw Anakin's face flush with embarrassment.

"Um, he isn't, uh . . . ," Anakin stammered. "That is to say, Ikrit isn't really my pet."

Tionne's face registered surprise, and her eyes swung toward Tahiri this time. "He's yours?" she asked in a shocked voice.

"Well, no," Tahiri said, "I—"

"What I meant to say is that he's not a pet," Anakin broke in. "Ikrit is actually a . . ."

Ikrit spoke. "I am a Jedi."

Uldir snickered. "The furball speaks. I was wondering why he'd been so quiet. Hey, I thought Jedi were supposed to have some special way to sense other Jedi. If Ikrit's really this powerful Jedi Master, how come Tionne couldn't sense him?"

Tionne gasped. "Jedi *Master*?"

The floppy-eared creature spread its paws and nodded, almost as if taking a bow.

"Not only that," Tahiri added helpfully, "he was a student of Master Yoda's just like Master Skywalker was."

Tionne's mouth hung open. Tahiri thought that if it hadn't been for the smile of wonder that pulled at the corners of her mouth, Tionne might have looked quite silly.

"But . . . I—," Tionne said. "I'm sorry I treated you like a pet, but why did you keep yourself a secret for so long?"

"Mmmm. Because my mission is a small one, a modest one. I do not want the attention or the honors that are due to a Jedi Master."

"Well, if you earned it, why not?" Uldir asked.

"Because there was a time five hundred years or more ago when I had great power. I thought myself too important. When I became so proud that I nearly killed a friend with my lightsaber over a petty disagreement, Yoda risked his life to stop me."

Uldir snorted. "If you were such hot stuff with a lightsaber, where is it then? Did your Master Yoda take it away and send you to bed without eating?"

Tahiri was starting to get annoyed with Uldir. His last comment may have been meant as a joke, but it sounded rude to her. Ikrit did not seem to notice the sarcasm, though.

"On the day I nearly misused it, I buried my lightsaber. Although I spent many more years in training before I became a Jedi Master, still I have never used a lightsaber since that day."

"Well, you *were* in hibernation for about four hundred years," Tahiri pointed out.

"True," the white-furred Jedi Master admitted. "That probably saved my life when the Emperor and Darth Vader were hunting down and killing all of the Jedi. It was my mission to free the spirits of the Massassi children from the golden globe that saved me then," Ikrit said.

Tionne, who loved Jedi stories, looked at him curiously. "You said you had a smaller mission now, Master Ikrit. What is it?"

"The boy has great power, even greater than my own," Ikrit said, nodding toward Anakin. Then the furry creature waved a paw toward Tahiri. "The Force of the girl combined with the boy's is a fearful power indeed. For now, I wish only to train them and watch over them."

Uldir rolled his eyes. "But I guess *I'm* not important enough for you to worry about?"

"Mmmm." Ikrit thought for a moment before speaking. "Yes. You are important enough. I will watch over you as well."

Maybe it was just because Uldir finally felt included, Tahiri thought, but she was glad to see him smile at this.

"Thanks, furball," Uldir said, giving the creature a playful salute.

Tionne looked hopefully at the Jedi Master. "Master Ikrit, you must know that I collect stories and legends of the ancient Jedi. If you wouldn't mind—if you have any time to spare from watching over these three—would you share some of your stories with me?"

Ikrit nodded, and his floppy ears swung back and forth. "You are a fine teacher and a good listener. It would be my pleasure."

Artoo-Detoo tweedled and bleeped from the copilot's station.

Tionne turned to look at the control panel for a moment. "It looks like it will be several more hours before we reach Vjun," she said. "Why don't we all try to get some sleep."

Tahiri leaned over and whispered to Anakin, "Just think . . . in only a few hours you'll see Darth Vader's fortress."

FOUR

"Wow! Doesn't look very welcoming, does it?"

Looking at the small, dark planet of Vjun, Anakin found himself agreeing with Uldir's comment.

"Maybe that was the idea," Tahiri said. "Kinda sends a shiver up my back just looking at it."

Anakin nodded absently. He wondered if the entire planet was really as eerie as it looked, or if they just felt uncomfortable because they knew Darth Vader himself had built a stronghold here.

Uldir shook his head. "It seems strange to me. I thought that Darth Vader was a really powerful Jedi and a Dark Lord of the Sith. Why would he want to come to such a tiny planet?"

"Size matters not," Ikrit reminded him.

"Well, for a 'tiny' world, it looks like there are some pretty good-sized storms down there," Tionne said. "Check your crash webbing, everyone. We're going in for a landing. Ready, Artoo?"

Artoo-Detoo beeped once for yes. Tionne nosed the *Lore Seeker* down into the atmosphere.

"Are you sure you know where this fortress place is?" Uldir asked.

High winds began to buffet the *Lore Seeker* as it descended, and Tionne took a moment to stabilize the craft before answering. "Master Skywalker gave me coordinates for what he says is the safest landing area near Bast Castle." The *Lore Seeker* shuddered and jolted, but Tionne held their course steady.

Anakin felt his stomach lurch. Landings in his father's ship, the *Millennium Falcon,* were usually much smoother than this. He glanced at his companions. Uldir's face had turned as pale as Ikrit's fur, and beads of sweat stood out on his upper lip.

Tahiri's eyes were shut, and her hands gripped the arms of the seat tightly. "I think I'm going to be sick," she said in a small voice.

Tionne's voice was grim. "Hang on, everyone, it's going to get even rougher before we land."

Although it was daytime, the sky grew darker around them as the ship plunged into a cluster of roiling storm clouds. The ship shuddered again, and lightning crashed outside the view-ports.

"This would be a fine opportunity to practice your Jedi relaxation exercises, my young friends," Ikrit pointed out. The small Jedi Master sounded completely calm.

Anakin was thankful for the reminder as high winds continued to jostle the ship. He began to feel better almost instantly. "You all right?" he asked Tahiri.

She nodded. "Better."

Anakin was glad to see that Uldir seemed to have relaxed as well. His face was no longer deathly pale, though he merely grunted when Anakin asked how he felt.

"Not much longer now," Tionne said. The *Lore Seeker* jerked sideways, and she steadied it. "It's only about fifty more kilometers to the landing area."

Ikrit said, "I wish to help, if you would not object. I cannot control the weather, but if you will show me our path, I can use the Force to steady your ship."

"Thank you, Master Ikrit. I would appreciate your assistance," Tionne said in a relieved voice. In less than a minute she had shown him the coordinates to Bast Castle and their flight path.

Then Ikrit closed his blue-green eyes and stretched one paw toward the front viewport in the direction of their flight. Instantly the *Lore Seeker*'s shuddering quieted.

Anakin could still feel some vibration when winds struck the ship or lightning flashed close by, but the tiny Jedi Master held the ship steady while Tionne piloted the *Lore Seeker* in a smooth descent to the landing area. As the craft folded its coppery wings and touched down with a gentle thump, Anakin, Tahiri, Tionne, and Uldir burst into cheers and applause.

"All right, I admit it," Uldir said. "I'm impressed."

Artoo-Detoo twittered and bleeped enthusiastically.

"Good work, everyone," Tionne said. "And a special thanks to both of my copilots."

"Well, let's get out and take a look at Darth Vader's fortress," Tahiri said.

Anakin suddenly had a strange feeling at the pit of his stomach again. While safe on Yavin 4, he had been very curious to see the fortress his grandfather had built. But now that he was here, he wasn't so sure. . . .

The area where they had landed was rocky and bare except for a few stunted trees, whose leafless branches stretched toward the cloudy sky. Anakin turned in a slow circle to look around. Dark rocky spires stretched up hundreds of meters to disappear into the mist and low clouds. But they saw no sign of any buildings. "Where is the castle?" he said at last.

Tionne sighed. "According to Master Skywalker, it's up there." She pointed to one of the rocky peaks. Tahiri, Anakin, and Uldir exchanged surprised glances. Distant lightning flickered across the shadowy landscape.

"Don't worry," Tionne said, "the information broker told me how to get to the top."

"Then why didn't we just fly up there?" Uldir asked.

"Master Skywalker warned me that the wind and storms might make it difficult for me to pilot the *Lore Seeker* safely onto the landing platform in front of Bast Castle. Even some modern ships have trouble making that landing."

"Did Uncle Luke tell you anything about the fortress itself?" Anakin asked. "I don't know much about it."

"Well, I found out as much as I could before we left. Apparently Vader built Bast Castle as one of his private strongholds; he was a powerful man. After both he and Emperor Palpatine died, some of the Emperor's followers brought a copy of Palpatine's body here—a clone. This second Emperor was defeated too. Since then, the fortress has been abandoned, as far as we know."

A cold rain began to drizzle down on the

gathered companions. And soon the wind picked up again, chilling them all.

"I still don't get it," Uldir said to Anakin. "Why would your grandfather choose to build in such a desolate place?"

Anakin's teeth were beginning to chatter. "Guess he didn't want many visitors."

Despite the freezing rain and her bare feet, Tahiri had clambered to the top of a rock to get a better view of their surroundings. Her feet looked blue from the cold and Anakin wondered if she really was more comfortable without boots on.

"Um, it looks like they still get at least *some* visitors," Tahiri said.

"What do you mean?" Anakin asked, climbing up beside her.

She pointed to a spot a hundred meters away, where a battered old cargo shuttle was half hidden in the shadow of a rocky outcropping. Lightning flashed, brightening the area around the small ship for a moment.

"Looks empty," Anakin said.

Tahiri nodded. "I wonder if it's been there very long."

The chilly rain stopped as suddenly as it had begun, but the wind still howled around them.

"I think we'd better get up to Bast Castle as soon as the weather improves," Tionne said. "I just hope we're not too late to find what we came for."

"Look," Tahiri gasped, and pointed upward.

The wind that had been making them all shiver had also broken up the clouds and pushed them aside. Towering above them, on a grim stony peak, sat Bast Castle.

The fortress was domed and heavily armored, with a craggy spike at the center. Dark and brooding, it looked like a deadly battleship hovering in the sky just above the tip of sharp rock that stabbed upward. Lightning flashed around it like blaster fire. Thunder rumbled.

"It's hard to imagine," Tahiri said, "that anyone ever called this place home."

FIVE

It was a dark and stormy day. Tahiri shivered as she looked out the *Lore Seeker*'s viewport at the rain and gusty winds that swept Vjun's bleak landscape. She yanked at a strand of her damp blonde hair. Now that they had all changed into dry clothes and eaten a warm meal, Tahiri was ready to face the climb up to the fortress. But the weather, if anything, had gotten worse. It was raining again—much harder this time— and her feet refused to get warm.

"Do you think it will let up?" Anakin asked.

"From what Master Skywalker told me, the weather on this planet is never very pleasant," Tionne said.

"I guess it's a good thing we brought thermal liners to wear under our jumpsuits then," Anakin said. "And our rain gear too."

"How long are we going to wait?" Uldir asked impatiently. "We don't know how long this rain will last. It could be days."

Tionne sighed. "That's true. Let's gather all of our equipment together and get our rain gear ready. We'll wait another hour. If it hasn't let up by then, we'll start anyway."

Tahiri looked down at her bare feet. They were still cold, and when she wriggled her toes she could hardly feel them. But she detested shoes, and her voice was miserable as she told Tionne, "I hate to say it, but I think I'll have to wear those soft boots you had made for me. I hope I'll only need them for the climb. Once we get to the castle I may take them off again, of course."

The Jedi teacher's face was solemn as she nodded at Tahiri and said, "Of course."

As it was, the rain eased up in half an hour, and the companions set out on foot toward the base of the rocky spire—all except Ikrit, who rode as usual on the dome of Artoo-Detoo's head.

Freezing winds curled around their legs like icy snakes as they walked. Tahiri shivered again and tried to think about something other than the cold. Her loose blonde hair whipped around her face. Her nose was starting to drip, and the chilly gusts stung her eyes and made her cheeks and ears numb.

"The information broker on Borgo Prime said there was a stairway around the back of the rock," Tionne said. "Ah, here we are."

Now that they were getting close, Anakin looked upward. "Will this lead us to the landing pad?" he asked.

Tionne inspected the stairway etched into the side of the rock pinnacle. "Not exactly. This takes us to the back of Bast Castle. The last time Master Skywalker was here, there were automatic lasers firing on anything that moved in front of the fortress. He knew about this rear stairway and suggested it might be safer."

"He probably just wanted us to be extra careful," Anakin said. "The stairs look pretty steep, Artoo," he added. "Can you make it?"

Artoo-Detoo warbled uncertainly.

"If he cannot, I will use the Force to help him over the rough parts," Ikrit said

Tahiri eyed the stairs warily. She spotted several broken steps with jagged edges. "Glad I'm wearing my boots after all," she muttered.

"What about you, Uldir?" Tionne asked. "Are you ready for the climb?"

The teenager shrugged and grinned. "Hey, this kind of stuff is why I wanted to be a Jedi

Knight. I came for adventure—and I'm ready for anything."

Anakin wasn't really surprised when it started raining again only a few minutes after they began their climb. Their protective clothing kept them dry for the most part. What surprised him was the *cold*. The rain was freezing.

The stairs to the fortress led up in a spiral that began outside, tunneled into the rock, and then wound back to the outside again as the stairs led higher. In and out, in and out. The icy rain made the stone steps slippery, and Anakin was glad each time the stairway tunneled back into the rock. Even though they stopped several times to rest away from the wind and rain, Anakin found himself growing tired.

"How—how much—farther—do you—think—it is?" Tahiri asked, collapsing beside Anakin during one of their rest breaks. In spite of her rain hood, bedraggled clumps of wet hair were plastered against her forehead and cheeks.

Anakin had no idea how far they had come, and he was too out of breath even to attempt an answer. He merely shook his head.

"I think we are about halfway," Tionne said. A healthy pink flush ran along the instructor's high cheekbones. She didn't seem to be breathing hard at all.

Uldir moved to the closest opening in the

stairway, leaned out, and looked up to the top of the rock spire. "She's right," he said. "We've got a long ways to go yet."

Tahiri groaned. "These stairs are giving me a headache."

Anakin closed his eyes and tried to convince himself that he felt much better after his brief rest.

"Among my people on the planet Kushibah," Ikrit said, "we have a proverb: The path to success is seldom short."

Uldir pulled his head back inside and crouched next to Anakin and Tahiri. "Yeah? I'll bet your people always go the long way around instead of taking shortcuts when they see them." The teenager wiped a hand across his cheek and came away with a fingerful of slush. He grinned. "I *thought* the rain outside felt awfully cold." He held out his finger to show Anakin. "Sleet. The rain has turned to sleet."

This time it was Anakin's turn to groan. He was already tired of being cold and damp.

Tionne's silvery brows drew together in a frown. "That means we'll all have to take extra care on the slippery steps outside," she said. "Especially Artoo."

Anakin pushed himself back to his feet and reached out a hand to help Tahiri up as well. "The sooner we get up to the castle the sooner we can get warm and dry," he said. "Ikrit and I will follow Artoo to make sure he doesn't slip."

Artoo-Detoo whistled a halfhearted agreement and they all set off again.

It was late in the day when the companions finally stood on a broad ledge at the rear entrance to Bast Castle, all somewhat the worse for wear. Anakin had a bruised knee and chin from having slipped and fallen heavily on the stairs. At least twice, Artoo-Detoo had teetered precariously at the edge of the steps before Ikrit had managed to use the Force to catch and lift him to safety. Tahiri had a scrape on one cheek from stumbling and falling against the rock wall.

And so it had gone for all of them. Cold, bone-weary, and aching from their climb, they wanted nothing more than to get out of the wind and rain for a while.

Tionne carefully raised one hand and waved it in front of the motion sensors beside the blast panel on the fortress door. "No laser blasts," she said. "That's a good sign. Maybe Imperials turned the defenses off when they left. Artoo, we'll need you to open the cyberlock on this door."

Buzzing and twittering, Artoo-Detoo rolled forward and put one of his probes into the computer-operated lock. The impressive double doors were five meters tall and almost as wide.

While waiting for the little droid to open the doors, Anakin and Tahiri backed up to get a better look at the fortress now that they were close enough to see it. Bast Castle looked to Anakin like an enormous armor-plated helmet with a large spiky tower rising from its center. Dark metallic blast shielding covered every wall and window.

Artoo-Detoo whistled in surprise and prodded the huge doors. They swung inward on noiseless hinges.

"Wow, that was fast," Tahiri said.

"Yeah, good work, Artoo," Anakin said.

Together, the two companions moved forward to get their first glimpse of the inside. Neither of them went in, but Anakin leaned through the broad doorway and looked around.

What he saw made him catch his breath. Ahead, in a room as big as the Grand Audience Chamber at the Jedi academy, lay the enormous black-robed figure of Darth Vader. It took Anakin a moment to realize that the plasteel helmet and black flowing cape were really part of a statue— a larger-than-life statue of Darth Vader that had been toppled to the floor, discarded like a piece of old junk.

Uldir shouldered his way into the entrance beside Anakin and pushed the gigantic portal open all the way. "It's cold out here. Why don't we go inside where it's warm and dry?"

Without warning, bright steaks of laser fire crisscrossed the courtyard.

"Stay back," Ikrit rasped.

"Everyone down," Tionne yelled.

Anakin, Tahiri, and Uldir hit the floor.

SIX

Another bright streak burned across the air in front of Anakin. "Blaster bolts!" Uldir yelped in his ear.

"Yeah, that's exactly what my brother Jacen always says," Anakin muttered. "Only this time they're lasers, not blasters."

"I think we set off some sort of intruder alarm," Tahiri said.

Uldir snorted. "You figured that out all by yourself, did you? Of *course* we set off an alarm—and now someone's shooting at us!"

"Not some*one*," Anakin corrected. "Some*thing*."

Uldir grunted. "Okay, fine. But whatever it is will probably come out here any minute and kill us."

"No," Ikrit said immediately. "I sense no life-forms, no intelligence in that room."

"Whatever it is, it isn't alive," Tionne agreed. "I can feel that."

"I think it's an automatic system," Anakin said. "Tahiri was right when she said we triggered something. It looks like some sort of intruder defense. It *must* be automatic. Look how regular the pattern is: two shots every second, first from the front left and right, and then from the rear left and right."

Laser bolts continued to streak across the entry hall and through the doorway. "Good deduction, Anakin," said Tionne.

"So what should we do?" Tahiri asked.

"I'm open to suggestions at this point," the Jedi teacher said, glancing over at her three charges.

Uldir gave Anakin a light nudge with his elbow. "You've figured it out this far. What's the solution?"

Anakin was surprised to hear Tahiri agreeing with Uldir. "He's right, you know, Anakin," she said. "I'm sure if you think of this as a puzzle to solve, we'll come up with an answer in no time."

Anakin looked over at Ikrit for some sort of support, but the old Jedi Master merely nodded as if to encourage him. Anakin thought, letting his eyes roll up and to one side. It came to him in just a moment. "Okay, Artoo," he said, "have you analyzed the pattern?"

The barrel-shaped droid beeped once.

"Do you think you can use that little mirror gadget that Uncle Luke installed in your head to deflect some of the laser bolts back so that one of us can get in and disable the lasers?"

"But that little mirror can't protect Artoo from blaster bolts," Tahiri objected. Her bright green eyes were wide with alarm.

"That's true," Anakin said. "But these are lasers. Lasers are just concentrated light. A mirror *can* deflect laser beams. Artoo should be fine—as long as he doesn't get shot."

Before Anakin could say any more, Artoo-Detoo beeped once again and rolled into action. Laser blasts shot toward the little droid as he trundled into the huge entry area. He reflected the first and second bolts back in the direction of the lasers that had shot them. To Anakin's surprise, one of the deflected blasts struck the laser that had fired it. The laser exploded with muffled sizzles and thumps. Artoo moved forward and caught the third bolt on his reflector as well.

"Stay here," Tionne ordered. As Artoo-Detoo reflected a fourth blast, Tionne and Ikrit sprinted into the vast entry hall and took cover behind the statue of Darth Vader. The fifth laser bolt struck the side of Artoo-Detoo's domed head and the droid let out an electronic shriek. Even so, the brave little droid swiveled to catch the next laser bolt.

"Hang on, Artoo," Tahiri cried.

"Tionne—your lightsaber!" Anakin called.

The Jedi teacher launched herself to her feet and ran toward Artoo-Detoo. With her first step, Tionne drew out her lightsaber and in one smooth motion ignited it. Letting the Force guide her movements, she drew the automatic laser fire and deflected several bolts while Ikrit used the Force to lift the little droid back to safety near the entrance. Artoo trundled to shelter behind one of the large doors.

Anakin crawled forward into the entryway on his stomach, dodging blasts of concentrated light.

"Stop! What are you doing?" Tahiri hissed.

"There must be a way to disarm the lasers," Anakin said, glancing back at his friend. "Something near the entrance, so the people who lived here could get in. I've got to find it."

"Well, you're not going without me, Anakin Solo!" Tahiri said and wriggled along the stones following him.

"No guts, no glory," Uldir agreed. He scrambled after them, ducking bolts of laser fire.

Ahead, Anakin could see that Tionne and Ikrit had begun flinging chunks of plasteel from the broken statue at the deadly lasers. He rolled to the left to avoid the sizzling beam of light that struck the floor by his head. His elbow thumped painfully against the huge door, but he got to his hands and knees and kept going until he could look around its edge and see the wall behind the door, where Artoo had taken shelter. To his right, Tahiri and Uldir were doing the same.

"There's nothing here!" Tahiri cried.

On the wall just above Artoo's head was a control panel. "I've got it!" Anakin yelled back.

With a bright flash, a laser hit the statue of Darth Vader near the spot where Ikrit and Tionne were working. A hunk of smoking plasteel broke off from the statue.

Anakin crawled around the huge door and pushed himself to his feet. He tried a few combinations to work the controls. Nothing happened.

Tionne hurled the still-smoking chunk of statue back at the lasers.

"I need your help, Artoo," Anakin said. The wounded droid gave a brave beep and plugged himself into the panel as another bolt of laser fire speared toward them.

Anakin hit the floor again. The laser blast caught Artoo on his right leg—but not before the astromech droid had finished his job. That was the last shot fired: All of the remaining lasers were disabled.

Groaning, Anakin got back to his feet. "Are you okay, Artoo?" he asked. "I'll be right back."

He went to the center of the doorway to check on Tahiri and Uldir. They were unhurt.

Tahiri blinked at Anakin in amazement. "That was a great solution."

Uldir clapped one hand down on Anakin's shoulder. "Not half bad for a kid," he said.

Anakin winced. His ribs felt bruised from diving to the floor so quickly, and his feet and legs ached from the long climb.

"Is it safe to go in now?" Tahiri asked.

"Wait there," Ikrit said.

While the Jedi Master and Tionne checked out the great entry hall, Anakin closed his eyes and tried to sense any danger in the area. He didn't detect any, but at the moment he couldn't tell if that meant there was no danger present or if it was simply too well hidden. After all, this fortress had belonged to Darth Vader, a Dark Lord of the Sith. Vader had been a powerful Dark Jedi. He might have set booby traps or other safeguards that Anakin couldn't sense. Traps that the Imperials who came to the castle later had not found or disarmed.

"It is safe to enter now," Ikrit said.

Although Anakin stood just inside the doorway, something held him back. *This place belonged to my grandfather,* he thought. *But never while he was Anakin Skywalker, the good man for whom I was named.* This had been Darth Vader's castle. He had built it, and he had lived there. *How can I go into this place?* Anakin wondered.

Tahiri had no such qualms, however. Neither did Uldir. Both of them stepped forward into the large chamber.

But still Anakin hung back. A biting wind whipped across the platform again, and blew through the doorway. He shuddered.

"Come on in," the sturdy teenager said. "It's a lot warmer in here."

Tahiri plopped herself on the floor just inside the entry. "I hope those were the last stairs we have to climb. My legs may never be the same again!" With a sigh of bliss, she pulled off the boots that Tionne had given her for their trip to Dagobah. "Much better," she declared.

Anakin thought back on what he had learned in the cave on Dagobah. His quest had taught him that he came from a mixed family—there were good Jedi and bad Jedi, smugglers and heroes. His grandfather was a part of him. But Anakin could choose what path he would take. He wouldn't let the ghosts of the past make his choices for him. Only *Anakin* would decide what kind of Jedi he would become.

Suddenly, his hesitation melted away, and Anakin walked into Darth Vader's fortress.

SEVEN

The smooth stone floor of the enormous chamber felt wonderful against Tahiri's bare feet. Even though freezing rain and howling winds raged outside, the polished rock floor inside the castle was warm.

Tahiri guessed that Anakin might need a few minutes alone to think, now that they were really here in the fortress his grandfather had built. It was impossible for her friend to forget that Anakin Skywalker had chosen to serve Emperor Palpatine and the dark side of the Force by becoming Darth Vader. Tahiri knew that Anakin had learned to live with those thoughts since their adventures on Dagobah. Even so, it was something he could never forget.

Tionne and Ikrit were looking for a way into the main rooms of the castle, so Tahiri got her sore legs moving again and went to help Uldir check on the damage to Artoo-Detoo. "Artoo, are you all right?" she asked.

Artoo-Detoo managed a weak bleep and turned to show her his damaged side.

"It doesn't look as bad as I expected," Uldir said, squatting down next to the little droid and looking at the laser-burned area.

Artoo-Detoo burbled a comment.

"I'm not sure what he's saying," Uldir said, "but I know a lot about fixing these little droids. My parents started teaching me how when I was about two years old." He swung open the damaged panel and peered inside.

"Really?" Tahiri asked doubtfully as she looked over his shoulder.

"Well, okay, I was older than two. But I *have* been around mechanics for most of my life," Uldir said. He pointed inside. "Looks like we burned out a few circuits here in the area that controls his right leg." Uldir made a few adjustments. "This is the best I can do without more tools. Artoo's leg won't move very well right now, but it's nothing I can't fix when we get back to Yavin 4."

"Hear that, Artoo?" Tahiri said, giving the little droid a pat. "You're going to be just fine." Artoo gave a happy-sounding tweet.

Tahiri was still concerned. "Are you sure?" she asked.

"Well, Artoo won't be able to climb any more stairs, but everything else is working fine," Uldir assured her.

"He's right," Anakin said, coming up behind Tahiri. "I can usually sense if the insides of machinery aren't working right. Those circuits there are the only problem. That was very brave, Artoo," Anakin said, addressing the droid directly. "We'll get you fixed up again good as new."

Ikrit and Tionne rejoined the group. "That was very quick thinking on your part, Anakin," said Tionne.

"I didn't really do much," Anakin objected. "You and Artoo did all the work."

Tionne gave her head a small shake. "I let the Force guide my actions, but you came up with the solution." Her pearly eyes twinkled and her smile was warm. "It's always a good skill for a Jedi to be able to think quickly under fire."

"Why *were* all those lasers firing at us, anyway?" Uldir asked. "I thought you said this place was abandoned."

"It has been for many years now," the instructor said. Her voice was uncertain, though.

"Then why were all those automatic defenses armed and ready?" Tahiri asked. "Why weren't they turned off?" She didn't like being shot at any better than the others did, and her curiosity now got the better of her. "I mean, I know you said that there might be lasers guarding the landing pad out front, but this is the *back* door. If no one lives here, why is this place so heavily defended?"

"I don't know," Tionne admitted.

"Probably to guard something valuable," Anakin said.

"Seems like an awful lot of firepower just to protect a broken statue and some old guy's lightsaber," Uldir scoffed.

Ikrit said, "Perhaps the last people to live here believed they would return, and so they left the security systems armed."

"It's possible that they never turned them off in the first place," Tionne suggested.

"Or maybe someone got to the fortress before we did and activated everything again," Uldir said.

"Well, one way or another," Anakin said, "I'm sure we'll find more defenses and booby traps the closer we get to whatever is most valuable here."

Ikrit nodded and gave a grunt. "The boy makes good sense. We must all be careful."

"When do we start looking for the lightsaber?" Tahiri asked, leaning over to massage her aching legs. "I hope there aren't any more stairs."

"The sooner we start, the better," Tionne answered. "If there's any chance someone else is here looking for the lightsaber, too, we should find it as quickly as we can and leave."

Tahiri got a tingly feeling at the back of her neck when she heard that. As tired as she was, she had a strange feeling that it was important for them to hurry. "Will it be faster if we split up?" she asked.

"No, I don't think so," Tionne said quickly.

"It may become necessary," Ikrit pointed out.

"For now," the silvery-haired instructor said, "I think we should all stick together."

After a brief rest and a light meal from the provisions in their packs, the companions began to explore. Several short hallways led away from the main chamber, though most of them only led to storage rooms and air ducts.

Tahiri had tucked her boots into her pack, and her bare feet padded noiselessly on the hard floor. Every room and hallway smelled slightly of rock and metal and plasteel, but the air that flowed from the ducts overhead was surprisingly fresh. Bright orange glowpanels lit their way wherever they went. In fact, all of the systems in the castle seemed to be in perfect working order.

Ikrit still rode atop Artoo-Detoo, but the droid

could not turn as well as he had before being pummeled by the laser blasts. Sometimes Ikrit got off to give the little droid a push and turn him back in the right direction.

They explored for an hour or so without finding their way into the main rooms of the castle. They found nothing of interest down any of the smaller hallways, and after each exploration they were forced to return to the huge room from which they had started.

Finally Tionne agreed to let the group split up, but only for a few minutes. "Anakin and I will take this hallway," she said, pointing to another small corridor. "Ikrit and Artoo will take the second one, and Uldir and Tahiri will search the next hallway over." She looked at her wrist chronometer. "Don't be gone long, though," she said. "Everyone meet back here by the statue of Darth Vader and report what you've found in five minutes."

"Okay," Anakin said.

Artoo-Detoo beeped a "yes." Ikrit nodded his agreement.

"Fine with me," Tahiri said.

Uldir flipped Tionne a playful salute. "Yes, captain. We'll see you here in five minutes."

With no time to waste, each pair set off. In less than five minutes all six of them were assembled again in the large chamber to compare their findings.

Tahiri tugged at a strand of her pale yellow hair as she listened to the others' reports.

"There were two storage rooms in our hallway," Anakin said. "The first one was open and empty, but the second one was locked."

Tionne nodded. "I managed to open it using my lightsaber."

"The whole storeroom was full of Imperial food rations," Anakin finished. "They're not very tasty, but we brought some along just in case we need them."

Uldir made a gagging sound. "Well, it'll have to be a real emergency before I eat any of those."

Tionne passed out the rations, and the companions stuffed them into the equipment packs they carried on their backs.

Ikrit and Artoo gave their report next. "Our hallway ended in a large circular room," the Jedi Master said in a scratchy voice. "It was empty except for some ankle and wrist irons chained to the wall." Artoo-Detoo gave a disapproving buzz. "I believe it was a place to hold prisoners for a short while when they were brought into the fortress," Ikrit said.

"Our hall was a bit nicer than that," Tahiri said. "More useful, at least—don't you think so, Uldir?"

The older boy nodded, and his face turned slightly red. "We, um, found a few old refresher units. They haven't been used in years, I guess, but they were clean and they worked just fine."

After the other companions had made use of the refresher units, the groups split up again.

This time the passage that Tahiri and Uldir took was wide and long. The smooth walls were unbroken by doorways, and the hall appeared to stretch out of sight ahead of them. Uldir picked up his speed. "That's a long way to go in five minutes," he said.

Suddenly Tahiri stopped still. "Wait," she said. "Don't go any farther. Something's wrong."

Uldir stopped and put his hands on his hips. "What now?" he asked.

"Something feels wrong," she answered.

"Like what?"

"The stone beneath my feet . . . it looks the same, but it—it feels rough. It feels *different*."

"That's *it*?" Uldir groaned in exasperation. "We have to turn back to meet the others in less than two minutes and you're worried about the floor being rough?"

"Yes. I mean no—I mean, it's more than that," Tahiri said. "Can't you *feel* it?"

Uldir stopped and ran his hand along the floor, feeling the texture. On hands and knees he crept forward, one arm outstretched. Then, all of a sudden he cried out and scrambled backward a few steps.

Tahiri rushed forward, afraid he was hurt. "What is it? What's wrong?"

Uldir was shaking and looking at his right hand. "It—it disappeared!" he said. "Right there. I stuck my hand out ahead of me and it disappeared. Then I pulled it back, and there it was again."

Tahiri sat beside him on the stone floor and looked at his hand. It seemed to be fine. She took the pack off her back, pulled out a heavy square packet of Imperial rations, and gingerly tossed it down the hallway ahead of them.

It disappeared completely—swallowed up by the floor. Uldir threw a package of rations. The packet vanished.

Then, a split second later, in a flash of sparks, the long hallway ahead of them disappeared as well. Instead of stretching into the distance, the passage came to a dead end at a flat metal wall. Between Tahiri, Uldir, and the wall was a wide, deep pit.

"It was a hologram!" Uldir said. "The whole hallway."

Together they crept to the edge of the pit and looked down. Ten meters below, the bottom of the pit was lined with sharp spikes as tall as Tahiri herself. The floor was littered with bones, and a packet of Imperial rations was speared on the tip of one spike. Tahiri felt a little queasy.

Uldir gulped and sat up. "I guess we'd better

go back and tell the others," he said. Both of them turned around to head back, and then froze—for there, snarling at them in the middle of the corridor, stood three of the most hideous creatures Tahiri had ever seen.

EIGHT

Standing by the fallen statue of Darth Vader, Anakin looked uneasily at his wrist chronometer. "Uldir and Tahiri should have been back by now," he said.

Artoo-Detoo made a soft wailing sound.

Tionne's silver brows drew together in a worried frown. "It's not like Tahiri to be late. Not unless . . ."

"Not unless she's in trouble," Anakin finished for her.

"Mmm. Then we should not delay," Ikrit said.

"I sent them down that hallway there," Tionne said, pointing toward one of the many wide corridors.

Without thinking, Anakin ran toward the

hallway. Ikrit bounded after him. "Caution, boy," the Jedi Master said. "If our friends are in trouble, we will not help them by rushing into the same danger. Let the Force guide you."

Anakin slowed to a walk. He could feel his face flush and he felt silly, because of course Master Ikrit was right.

Tionne and Artoo caught up with them a moment later as they stood looking down the long bare corridor. "But . . . it's empty! I was sure this was the passage I sent them to explore," Tionne said.

"The hallway looks pretty long," Anakin said. "Maybe it branches off somewhere. Anyway, I can *feel* that this is where they are."

Ikrit's floppy ears stood up straight and he closed his blue-green eyes. "Yes, this is the way they came," he said.

All of a sudden a loud growl rolled up the hallway toward them. Anakin heard Tahiri scream, "Help!" She sounded close by, but he still couldn't see her.

"All right, let's go," said Tionne. "But be careful: something is definitely not right about this corridor."

They had taken only a few steps down the hallway when everything seemed to change around them. Anakin could now see the end of the corridor only ten meters away. Between him and the end of the corridor were Tahiri and Uldir.

Unfortunately, between them and Anakin were three snarling beasts of a kind Anakin had never seen before. Each of the scaly six-legged beasts had a ridge of spikes that ran along the back of its head and down its snout. Spines bristled all over their short heavy tails. Their scaly skin looked as if it was covered with reddish-brown rust, and their bellowing, growling voices sounded rusty too. Saliva dripped between double rows of sharp teeth as the creatures snapped at Tahiri and Uldir.

Anakin stood perfectly still. "What are they?" he asked Tionne. He tried desperately to use the Force to send a calming message to the animals, but they ignored him.

"They look like drakka boars from Randon," Tionne said. "The traders from that planet use these creatures to guard their greatest treasures."

Anakin shouted to his friends above the roars and snarls of the drakka boars. "Can you move farther away from them?"

"No room," Uldir shouted back.

"There's a deep pit behind us," Tahiri added.

Anakin groaned. "I wish I were as good at using my mind to talk with animals as my brother Jacen is. I tried to quiet their minds, but those drakka boars don't seem to hear me."

Ikrit spoke. "I have the gift of speaking to beasts, as your brother does. I too have tried to contact them, but their minds do not hear."

Tionne closed her eyes and concentrated. "Those can't be drakka boars, then," she said finally. "These creatures are always mind-linked to their masters, but I can't sense any minds at all."

"Nor I," Master Ikrit said.

The guard animals snarled and moved closer to Uldir and Tahiri, who took a few steps backward.

"If none of us can reach their minds," Anakin said, "then maybe they don't have minds we can reach."

"That's it!" yelled Uldir. "Just like the hallway!"

"You mean holograms!" Tahiri gasped. "Anakin, is there a way to find out if the beasts are holograms?"

"Artoo, can you shine a bright light at those drakka boars?" Anakin asked.

Artoo-Detoo tweedled and bleeped. A moment later the little droid shot a brilliant beam of light up the corridor. The drakka boars did not cast shadows. Instead, their outlines became dim and the bright light passed directly *through* them.

"They are not real," Ikrit said. "These holograms were put here to make us afraid."

Uldir snorted. "Well, it worked, furball. We were definitely scared."

"Do you think it's safe to come out, then?" Tahiri asked.

"Just a moment," Tionne said.

Drawing her lightsaber, the instructor switched it on and moved slowly up the hallway toward the pale holograms. She held perfectly still for a moment and then, with a move so fast Anakin could hardly see it, she slashed upward. Something gave a loud pop and sparks sprayed down from the ceiling around Tionne. The images of the drakka guard boars flickered and went out. In fact, all the holograms were gone now.

"That holographic projector won't be able to fool us again," Tionne said with a nod of satisfaction.

"And we have also learned something," Ikrit said.

"You mean that we should trust our Jedi senses and not just our eyes and our ears?" Anakin asked.

"That is true enough," Ikrit said. "But remember that the more tricks and traps we find, the closer we are to the treasures your grandfather wished to guard."

"Then that would mean—," Tahiri began.

"Look," Anakin said. He went over to the wall and traced his finger along the outline of a doorway that had been hidden by the hologram.

Placing a hand against one side of the stone door, he pushed. It budged. He pushed again, but nothing more happened.

"Do you think there's a password or an access code?" Tahiri asked.

Then, without quite knowing why, Anakin pressed one hand against the door and said, "I am Anakin. Let me in."

Without a creak or groan, the door swung open.

Carefully, checking for traps as they went, Anakin, Tahiri, Uldir, Tionne, Artoo, and Ikrit entered the tiny secret chamber. The small room was perfectly round, with a high domed ceiling. A soft bluish light radiated from the walls. There was nothing in the room except at the very center. There, in a ray of bright white light, stood a crystal column as clear as water.

On the very top of the column, about at Anakin's eye level, lay a lightsaber.

Glancing at Tionne and Ikrit to make sure that it was okay, Anakin reached out and took the hilt of the lightsaber in his hand. The handle felt warm and heavy and perfectly balanced. It was solid and well used, but not ancient.

Anakin knew he wasn't ready to be trained with a lightsaber yet, but this one held a special interest for him. Obi-Wan Kenobi had been

Darth Vader's Jedi teacher, and his uncle Luke's first teacher, too. Anakin ran a finger up the ridged handle and over the power stud, but did not press it.

"Here," he said, handing it to Tionne. "I think this is what we came for."

Tionne smiled and took it from him. "It was the weapon of a great Jedi."

"Mmm. It is better that such things never fall into the wrong hands," Ikrit said.

Just then Artoo-Detoo beeped an alarm.

At the same moment, a puff of smoke erupted in the doorway, and a dark-haired man with a neat beard, tawny eyes, and a deep purple cloak stood before them. The man threw back his head and laughed, although Anakin couldn't see what was so funny.

"The powerful Mage of Exis Station thanks you," he said. "I would never have found the lightsaber without your help." He snatched the weapon from Tionne's hand. "But I'll take it now."

NINE

As usual, Tahiri's curiosity got the better of her. It didn't occur to her until much later that she should have been terrified of this strange dark man brandishing a lightsaber. "Who are you?" she asked. "How did you get here? And why did you take that lightsaber? Only Jedi use lightsabers, and you don't look like a Jedi. You're not going to kill us, are you? Well, aren't you going to say anything?"

Every eye in the room turned toward Tahiri. Anakin coughed a couple of times, his brows raised in surprise. Tionne and Ikrit remained silent, but Artoo-Detoo gave a loud shrill of alarm. Uldir let out a low whistle.

The strange man blinked rapidly several times,

as if trying to think of the proper thing to say. "I—well, I . . ." Then he seemed to recover from his surprise. "Behold," he boomed in a rich voice, "I am the Mighty Orloc. Who are you?" He drew himself up to his full height and pulled back the hood of his deep purple cloak. The silver spangles along its edge glittered in the soft blue light.

Tionne's hair glowed silver-blue as she gazed calmly at the newcomer. "We'll be happy to introduce ourselves to you, 'Mighty' Orloc, if you'll be polite enough to give our lightsaber back. We need to take it to the Jedi academy to share with the other Jedi and students."

The strange man ignored her and continued in a louder voice. "I am the invincible Mage Orloc of Exis Station, and I claim this lightsaber as my rightful weapon. It is a fitting blade for—"

"Mage?" Tahiri interrupted. "You mean like a magician?" Out of the corner of her eye, Tahiri could see that Ikrit had climbed up onto Tionne's shoulder and was whispering something in her ear.

"I . . . ," Orloc seemed to have forgotten what he was about to say. He blinked furiously again and then recovered. "Yes, I am the most powerful Mage in all the Galaxy, and—"

"But magic is just tricks," Tahiri said. "Tionne and Ikrit are real Jedi. If you're only a magician, you don't know how to use the Force."

Orloc waved a hand, dismissing her comment. "No, I did not need to learn such things as they teach at your Jedi academy. I studied on my own.

"I have magical powers far greater than your puny Jedi tricks," Orloc went on, clutching the lightsaber handle to his chest.

"But you *aren't* a Jedi," Tahiri persisted. "And a lightsaber is a Jedi's weapon."

At the edge of her vision she saw Ikrit and Tionne with their eyes closed. She guessed that they were reaching out with the Force toward the Mage's mind, perhaps to pull the lightsaber from his grasp.

But whatever their plan, Orloc had already made his move. The lightsaber was no longer anywhere in sight, and the Mage's face grew stormy. "I have need of it," he said.

"Then why don't you build a lightsaber of your own, like Jedi do?" Anakin asked in a reasonable voice.

"Silence, fool!" Orloc thundered, pointing at Anakin with one hand. Fire flickered at the Mage's fingertips, but it was not the electrical energy that came with extreme power from the dark side of the Force. It was something Tahiri had never seen before.

The Mage took a step backward toward the rounded wall. He gave a bark of laughter. "With my powers I see and know many things you do not," he said.

Orloc's hand shot out and touched something on the wall, and instantly one of the flagstones beneath Tionne's feet turned downward at a sharp angle, forming a kind of slide or chute. Taken by surprise, Tionne lost her balance, fell to the flagstones, and slid out of sight into the darkness, with Ikrit still on her shoulder. Then, without a sound, the flagstone slipped back into place, leaving the floor as smooth and solid as it had been before. It had all happened in only a second or two.

Tahiri cried out.

"What did you do with them?" Uldir yelled, his voice cracking with anger.

Anakin rushed forward and pushed against the floor at the point where Tionne and Ikrit had disappeared. Tahiri ran toward the Mage with the idea of grabbing the lightsaber and forcing Orloc to help them find Tionne and Ikrit. But before she could reach him there was a blinding flash of light.

Thick white smoke ballooned up from the spot where Orloc had been standing. His laughter rang through the room. Tahiri reached out her arms to grab his cloak, or his leg, or whatever she could get ahold of, but there was nothing there.

By the time the smoke cleared, Tahiri, Anakin,

Uldir, and Artoo were completely alone. The three junior Jedi exchanged worried glances.

"Are . . . are they dead?" Uldir asked in a tone that said he feared the worst.

"No," Tahiri said right away. "I would have felt it through the Force."

Anakin shook his head as well. "I can sense them. They're still here in the castle somewhere."

Artoo beeped mournfully.

"Don't worry," Anakin said, "we'll find them." He sounded solid and sure.

"Of course we will," Tahiri said, taking heart from Anakin's confidence.

"It's a big castle," Uldir said doubtfully. "Who knows how many more Mages or pirates might be around?"

Tahiri gulped. She hadn't thought of that. "The Force will guide us to Tionne and Ikrit," she said more confidently than she felt.

"But shouldn't we be looking for that magician guy Orloc first?"

"Why?" Tahiri asked.

Uldir shrugged. "To get the lightsaber back before he has a chance to escape with it. The lightsaber is awfully important to Tionne. Isn't that why we came here in the first place?"

Artoo-Detoo gave a sad beep of agreement.

"Uldir and Artoo are right," Anakin said. "This may be our only chance to get the lightsaber back before it's gone forever. But what about Ikrit and Tionne?"

Uldir narrowed his eyes and looked at them shrewdly. "They're Jedi, aren't they? They can take care of themselves better than we can."

"Let's start searching for Orloc and the lightsaber," Tahiri suggested. "Tionne and Ikrit will probably find us along the way—or we'll find them."

"Well, yes . . . ," Anakin said with a frown. He stood and walked over to the panel by the door that the Mage had used. He closed his eyes for a moment and ran his fingers along it, then nodded and pushed a button.

One of the flagstones in the floor fell away sharply. The companions gathered around the hole.

"I knew these Imperial rations would be good for something," Anakin muttered. He threw another packet of rations down the hole to check it for depth. It landed a long, long way down. Anakin sighed. "There's too much of a drop, so we can't follow Tionne and Ikrit anyway. One of us might get hurt if we tried." He nodded. "All right. We'll go after the lightsaber first."

Artoo-Detoo beeped mournfully.

Tahiri put a comforting hand on the little droid. "It's okay, Artoo. We'll find Ikrit and Tionne *and* get the lightsaber back."

TEN

Tionne opened her eyes to total darkness. A voice came out of the inky shadows beside her.

"Are you well, my friend?"

"Yes. Thank you, Ikrit. Nothing is broken, but my body feels like it's covered with one giant bruise."

"That was a long fall," Ikrit said. "You used the Force well to control your slide and land with so little harm to your body."

"You must have controlled your own fall fairly well," Tionne responded. "You don't sound like you were hurt."

"True." The furry Jedi Master cleared his throat and sounded a bit embarrassed. "But you

75

cushioned my fall. I believe the bruise on your shoulder will be Ikrit-shaped."

"Oh! Is *that* why it feels like an Imperial chicken walker stepped on my shoulder?" Tionne groaned. "Where do you think we are?"

Ikrit gave a wheezing chuckle. "I could use the Force to sense what is around us," he said dryly, "but it might be simpler if we used light."

"I must have fallen harder than I thought," Tionne said ruefully, unclipping her lightsaber from her belt and turning it on. With a *snap-hiss,* the beautiful glowing blade sprang forth, shedding a bright pearly glow on their surroundings.

They were in a small room with rough stone walls and an uneven rock floor. A narrow metal staircase ran up one wall and vanished into darkness above.

"Can you walk?" Ikrit asked. "We must find our young Jedi friends."

Tionne got to her knees and then to a squatting position. She tested her weight on her legs before standing up completely. "I think so," she said in an unsteady voice.

"Mmm. Either you can walk or you cannot," Ikrit said. "Thinking will not help us reach the children."

Tionne thought about the junior Jedi somewhere above them in the castle with a strange man who claimed to be a magician and who was certainly a thief and possibly worse. "Yes, of course I can walk. 'Do or do not: there is no try,' as Master Skywalker always says."

Ikrit nodded. "These were Master Yoda's words as well." He began to climb the steep steps that ran along the wall. "We will find our friends, and we will get the lightsaber back. Who knows—by the time we track them down, the young ones may have found the Mage for us already."

"Yes," Tionne said thoughtfully, "that's exactly what worries me."

"I don't believe Orloc has any real magic," Anakin said, "so he can't have gone far."

"Then there's no time to lose," Uldir said, dashing out into the hallway and looking both directions for some sign of the Mage. Anakin and Tahiri followed him out, and Artoo-Detoo trundled after them.

"There," Tahiri said, pointing at the floor. Anakin looked down and saw the outline of a sooty boot print.

"He must be heading back toward the room where the statue is," Uldir said.

Artoo-Detoo warbled excitedly.

"All right, let's go," Tahiri said.

Together they ran to the end of the corridor, but they found no more footprints.

"Which way now?" Uldir asked. "Can you sense anything?"

Anakin saw Tahiri close her eyes. He closed his own eyes and reached out with the Force.

"No, I can't sense him," Tahiri said.

Anakin opened his eyes. "Neither can I." He heard a distant slapping sound.

"Sounds like someone running on stone," Tahiri said.

"It came from this direction," said Uldir, heading at a brisk trot down one of the corridors they had not yet explored.

Anakin and Tahiri dashed after him. Artoo-Detoo, tweeting and bleeping encouragement, followed as fast as he could with the damaged circuits in his right leg. Before long they came to a branching point in the corridor. Straight ahead of them a broad stairway rose at a sharp angle, while off to the left a small squarish tunnel led away to some other part of the castle.

"I'll bet he went this way," Uldir said, pointing toward the tunnel.

"Are you sure?" Tahiri asked.

Uldir snorted. "Of *course* not. I could be wrong, but we don't have time to waste talking about it. Now if *I* were Orloc, I'd go this way."

Anakin nodded. "You go that way then; we'll take the stairs."

"You've got to be kidding," Tahiri groaned. "Not the stairs. I can't take any more stairs."

Artoo-Detoo, who had just caught up with them, tweedled and buzzed noisily.

"Oh, no!" Tahiri said. "Artoo isn't in any condition to climb stairs."

Anakin looked at Artoo. "You'll have to go with Uldir then," he said, pointing toward the tunnel the older boy had taken. Artoo-Detoo beeped in agreement and rolled off down the tunnel.

As he and Tahiri began the climb up the stone staircase, Anakin gritted his teeth for a second, trying not to think of how sore his legs were going to be. The stairs offered no landings or flat areas on which to rest, or even any railings to hold on to, and there was a steep drop on either side of the solid rock staircase.

"Didn't—your grandfather—ever hear—of turbolifts?" Tahiri gasped as they climbed.

Anakin nodded. "Sure. We just—haven't found them—yet," he panted.

When they finally reached the top of the steps, Anakin's and Tahiri's legs shook with exhaustion, and perspiration streamed down their faces.

Before them was a single doorway. Tahiri leaned against the cool stone wall beside it, catching her breath while Anakin studied the door. With its rounded corners, armor plating, and multiple locks, the door looked as if it belonged on some ancient treasure vault. "If Orloc's up here, there's nowhere else he could have gone," Anakin said.

"Is the door locked?" Tahiri asked. To their surprise, it wasn't. It opened easily at Anakin's touch.

Anakin and Tahiri each tossed a packet of food rations inside to test for booby traps. No lasers fired, no trapdoors opened, no holographic guard beasts snapped and snarled.

Neither of them was prepared for what they saw when they stepped inside. A spacious chamber greeted them. Elegantly simple, the room held no ornaments of any kind. The floor and walls and ceiling were tiled completely with glossy black stone. Low benches of the same black stone reflected purplish light from the glowpanels set into the walls every few meters.

"What's this?" Tahiri asked, pointing to a raised platform that held a huge tube made of black plasteel. Wires and hoses snaked out from the cylinder in all directions. She ran a hand along its smooth side and found some sort of control panel.

"This looks like the tubes they use to bury dead people in space," Anakin said.

Tahiri pushed a button, and the cylinder split open with a *whoosh*. Anakin gasped. He and Tahiri exchanged astonished looks.

"This must have been his . . . his bedroom," Anakin said.

"You mean he slept in there?" Tahiri asked.

"But why would he need all those connectors and hoses?"

Anakin remembered what his parents and his uncle Luke had told him. "My grandfather's body was so damaged and scarred that he needed machines to keep him alive." Anakin shuddered. He wasn't sure he wanted to be reminded of all the evil things his grandfather had done, or that he had been almost half machine before he died.

Seeing another control panel in the lid of the bed unit, Anakin guessed Darth Vader must have used it to open or close the chamber. He reached out to touch the keypad on that control panel to shut the cylinder again, but it didn't close.

For a moment nothing happened, and then an image flickered in the air, hovering over the center of the bed. Something clicked and whirred, and a tiny hologram appeared, no bigger than Anakin's hand.

Tahiri grabbed Anakin's arm, a look of amazement on her face. "Why would Darth Vader keep a hologram of Master Skywalker?"

Anakin opened his mouth to speak, but nothing came out. The little hologram of a young Luke Skywalker turned in a slow circle, so that they could see it from every angle. "I think . . . ," Anakin finally said, "I think it's because Luke was his son."

"Then why isn't there a hologram of your

mother when she was Princess Leia?" Tahiri asked. "She was his daughter, wasn't she?"

Anakin frowned and nodded. "But Darth Vader didn't know about her until just before he died. He knew about Uncle Luke for a long time, though."

Anakin felt a lump form in his throat. "My mom keeps holograms of me and Jacen and Jaina on her desk at work, and Dad has one of me and the twins in the *Millennium Falcon*. I think Darth Vader was just doing the same thing."

"So maybe he wasn't all bad," Tahiri said in a soft voice.

"You may be right," Anakin whispered. "Uncle Luke was the one who helped him turn back from the dark side before he died, you know."

For the first time since they had reached Bast Castle, Anakin was very glad that he had come.

ELEVEN

Uldir raced down the tunnel at full speed, intent on catching the thief Orloc. Something about the lightsaber called to Uldir. In his mind, there was something almost magical about it. And he knew the other Jedi would be impressed if *he* managed to get the blade back from Orloc, all on his own.

Lightsabers had always been the weapons of the Jedi, and this one had belonged to a famous Jedi, Obi-Wan Kenobi. Somehow, deep inside, Uldir thought that maybe if he could get the lightsaber back and hold it, turn it on, it might awaken in him the Jedi powers that he was searching for.

His muscles still ached from the long climb up

to Bast Castle, but Uldir turned off the part of his mind that felt pain. He concentrated on his goal—getting that lightsaber back. He *had* to have it.

Uldir heard an electronic squeal behind him. "I can't slow down, Artoo," he called. "If you don't catch up to me before I find Orloc, I'll come back for you."

The little droid beeped once to show he understood.

Uldir continued to pelt down the tunnel. He couldn't tell for sure how far he had run. It seemed like at least half a kilometer before the tunnel broadened and fed out into a bright, high-ceilinged room. Moving more carefully now— and watching for holographic traps—Uldir entered. Inside were a dozen land speeders and air speeders, a couple of Imperial shuttles, and three beautiful spaceships that must have been hundreds of years old.

Uldir guessed he had found the docking bay at the front of Bast Castle. He decided to be bold. "Come out and show yourself. I know you're there," he said, although he knew no such thing. "I am a Jedi; you cannot hide from me."

It was a bluff, but it worked.

The Mage Orloc stepped out from behind one of the Imperial shuttles. "All right, you've found me," the Mage said. "Now, what do you plan to *do* with me? I am the Mage of Exis Station, and unless I miss my guess, *I* have a lightsaber and *you* do not."

To prove his point, Orloc held out the weapon and turned it on. Even in the well-lit hangar bay the pale blue beam appeared bright.

Uldir looked longingly at the glowing blade. He wanted so badly to hold it, to try it. Master Skywalker had said Uldir showed very little Jedi potential. But Uldir would prove to Luke Skywalker and the rest of them that it wasn't true. "What's it like?" he asked finally.

"So." The Mage looked shrewdly at the teenager and chuckled slightly. "You're not really a Jedi, are you?"

Uldir shook his head and took a step closer.

"But you want to be one," the Mage guessed.

Uldir nodded.

"To answer your question, the lightsaber feels wonderful," Orloc said, turning the blade this way and that—although it seemed to Uldir that the magician was rather clumsy at using the weapon. "This is *true* power," the Mage went on. His hand shook slightly as he drew an arc in the air with the glowing blade.

Uldir was surprised and took a step backward again. "Are you *sure* you know how to use one of those?"

Orloc faltered for a moment, blinked his tawny eyes several times, and then recovered. "Why, yes. Of course. Why, if you're truly interested, I could teach you the mysteries of the galaxy. Come with me to Exis Station. I'll teach you everything you need to know to become more powerful than a Jedi. You don't really need to study hard, you know. There's an easier way. I'll show you."

Uldir was definitely more interested than he wanted to admit. He had always suspected that there were easier ways of learning to use power. He thought for a moment. "You mean, you could teach me to lift that crate?" he asked, pointing to a box near an Imperial shuttle.

"Why, boy, I could teach you to lift that entire shuttle," Orloc said.

"Could you teach me to sense the thoughts of people?"

"Sense them?" Orloc said, laughing. "Why, I could teach you to read their minds just like a computer display screen."

Uldir found that hard to believe. If the Mage could read thoughts so easily, wouldn't he know what Uldir was thinking right now—that Orloc must be exaggerating? But the Mage *did* seem to know a lot. He might know something worth learning. Some shortcuts, perhaps. After all, Orloc had outwitted two grown Jedi and a few Jedi trainees with his magic, hadn't he? "How do you know so much about this place—the passages and trapdoors?"

"Three reasons." The Mage swirled his cape

out, bowed, and flashed a knowing smile. "First of all, I'm incredibly powerful. Second, I have great skill with mechanical things. Third, I also located a map of the fortress in a maintenance bay just after I arrived here. My special powers helped me to use the plans and the castle's own defenses to dispose of my . . . enemies."

Uldir frowned at the boast. Now he wanted to see how far the Mage was willing to go. "And of course you could teach me to use a lightsaber."

"Of course," the Mage agreed. "And to build your own."

Aha, Uldir thought. *Orloc can hardly* hold *a lightsaber. I doubt that he could teach me to use one.*

But before he could speak, Orloc continued. "Why, my boy, once I find the other object I came here for, I'll teach you—"

"What other object are you looking for?" Uldir interrupted.

"Why, the Holocron, of course, lad. And once I get to Vader's private quarters and take the Holocron out of its special vault, I'll be able to teach you anything—*anything at all*—about being a Jedi. With that and my own magic, we'll be invincible. We can conquer any power in the galaxy."

Now Uldir was interested again. "What's so special about this Holocron thing?" he asked.

"It contains all the recorded lessons of a great Jedi Master."

Uldir wavered. "I don't know. If two living Jedi Masters can't teach me to use the Force, I'm not sure that a Jedi recording in a box could do it." He looked again at the clumsy way the Mage held the lightsaber. "And if you don't have any Jedi powers, that thing probably won't help *you* much," he said. "Why don't you leave the lightsaber with me so I can give it to a real Jedi, someone who can use it?" His voice squeaked at the end of his speech, ruining the effect of his brave words.

Orloc shook his head. "Doesn't quite fit in with my plans, *boy*. Either come with me to Exis Station and learn what I can teach you . . . or, if you won't join me"—he took a step toward Uldir and waved the lightsaber menacingly— "why, I'll be forced to consider you an enemy."

The Mage took another step closer. "And I've found that if my enemies want what I have, it's never wise to let them live."

TWELVE

Tahiri sighed and looked down the seemingly endless corridor. "Well, at least it's not stairs anymore," she muttered to herself.

"I sure hope Uldir's all right," Anakin said.

"Me too. I have a feeling he's in some sort of trouble," Tahiri said, and quickened her pace. Both she and Anakin had wanted to explore Vader's private chambers further, but once it was clear that the Mage was not hiding there, they knew they would have to continue their search elsewhere, and quickly.

"I think we're headed the right way, though," she said. "This corridor runs the same direction as the one Uldir took. And I think I can feel him up ahead of us somewhere—though I can't really sense him as well as I can sense you. I suppose that comes from knowing you so much better." She chattered on, covering her worry with a stream of words. "But once we find Uldir and Artoo, we'll still have to find Orloc, and once we find him and get the lightsaber back, there's Tionne and Ikrit to locate too."

The passageway grew wider and they could see a bright light not too far ahead. Anakin glanced at her with one eyebrow raised. "You forgot to mention what comes after we find Tionne and Ikrit," he said.

"What's that?" she asked.

"We'll need to get back to the ship."

"Oh no," Tahiri moaned. "More stairs."

They were almost to the end of the corridor when Anakin stopped short and held up one hand, as if listening. Tahiri stopped talking and listened too.

Voices. She heard voices. They sounded far away, but she was certain one of them belonged to Uldir. She mouthed his name silently at Anakin. He nodded.

A loud laugh rang out.

"And Orloc," Anakin whispered.

Pressing a finger to her lips, Tahiri carefully crept forward into the light. Anakin stayed close beside her. Soon they found themselves on the topmost level of a gigantic, airy room, three stories high. Keeping their heads down, Anakin

and Tahiri crawled over to the edge of the walk-
way onto which they had emerged. Far beneath
them, on the bottom level, stood the purple-
robed Orloc with Obi-Wan Kenobi's lightsaber,
waving it back and forth at Uldir.

"We'll have to help him," Anakin whispered.

Tahiri nodded. "Is there a turbolift?" she whispered back. She looked around the high metal
catwalk and saw to her dismay that the only
way to the bottom level was down a dozen
flights of metal mesh steps. A network of plasteel poles supported the slender stairway.

"I'm not sure we can make it down there in
time," Anakin said, looking at the stairs.

"Oh, yes we can," Tahiri said. "We're a team,
remember? I have an idea, but there's no time to
explain. You make a distraction and then follow
my lead. I just hope Orloc doesn't have a blaster."

"I don't think he does," Anakin said. "If he did,
he would have had it out and aimed at us when
he stole the lightsaber."

"I sure hope you're right," Tahiri said. She
scrambled quietly to the head of the staircase
and looked down. The very sight of the steps
made her feel queasy, but they *had* to save
Uldir. She nodded back toward Anakin, and
right on cue he stood up and began yelling.

"Hey, Orloc!" he shouted. "Up here! If you hurt
Uldir, you'll be making a big mistake, you know."

It worked.

The thin Mage with the long dark hair turned and looked up to where Anakin was standing. This was the chance Tahiri had been waiting for. She pulled herself up onto the stair railing on the side away from the Mage and swung herself over it. Holding on to the rail with both hands, she wrapped her aching legs around one of the tall poles that supported a corner of the staircase. Then, using her teeth, she yanked the sleeve of her flightsuit up over one hand to protect it and let go of the railing with the other. Tahiri whizzed down the smooth pole, controlling her speed by tightening or loosening her grip.

Anakin kept Orloc's attention, and in seconds Tahiri had reached the floor. Her legs felt so weak, they almost refused to hold her up when she touched down, but she hung on to the pole with both hands to steady herself.

Tahiri peeked around the edge of the stairway toward the Mage. She let her eyes fall half closed and tried to visualize pulling the lightsaber from his hand. She had often managed to lift pebbles and leaves and even heavy objects during training, but not usually while someone was holding them—or while someone was moving the objects around, for that matter. This time she couldn't manage it.

Orloc must have felt the tug at his weapon, because he gave a surprised shout and grasped the hilt with both hands. Tahiri ducked back behind the stairway.

"Time for the backup plan," she muttered to herself. Oh, how she wished that Tionne and Ikrit were with them. Well, until they arrived it was up to her and Anakin to rescue Uldir and the lightsaber. She decided to rely on the things she *knew* she could do, so she resorted to one of her strongest weapons: talking.

"Mage Orloc, put down your weapon," she said, stepping out into plain view. She had to keep the Mage busy long enough for Uldir to get out of his reach. "None of us means you any harm. We only want the lightsaber you took, because it's very special to us."

The Mage turned his tawny eyes toward Tahiri, and Uldir began backing carefully away from him. Encouraged, Tahiri continued talking. "And even if you have some kind of magic, that lightsaber won't be worth much to you without Jedi powers, without the Force to guide you."

Tahiri heard a soft thump as Anakin slid down one of the stair supports and landed behind her.

"Why, that's a nice story, little girl," Orloc said with a harsh laugh. "But I have special plans—and they include a lightsaber. I see no reason to give this one up when I have it right here in my hand." He lowered the blade so that it pointed directly at Tahiri and swung it back and forth a few times. He could not control it very well. It bobbed and wobbled in the air. Uldir backed farther away.

Good, Tahiri thought, *Uldir is almost safe.* But then she realized that *she* was in trouble now, even if Orloc only meant to frighten her. He was so unskilled with the lightsaber that she might truly be in danger. Suddenly a small crate drifted through the air and bumped Orloc's arm.

Startled, the Mage slashed with his lightsaber blade and then gaped in surprise when the little carton dropped to the floor in two smoking pieces. He fell back a few paces and stared at it. Then another carton drifted toward him.

Tahiri got the idea. Anakin must be using the Force to lift simple objects. The second crate nudged the Mage a bit harder.

Tahiri heard a low warble in back of her and realized that Artoo-Detoo had found his way into the hangar bay. "We don't want to hurt you, Mage Orloc," she said, comforted to know that Anakin and Artoo were just behind her, hidden by the stairway.

Orloc slashed at the second box. "Why, fortunately, I'm not limited by such small thoughts. I'm going to leave here with this lightsaber, and I'm ready to hurt *you* to do it."

Suddenly Tahiri heard a *whoosh* like the sound of a lightsaber being ignited. "I'm afraid I can't let you do that," the Jedi teacher Tionne's voice said from behind Orloc.

The Mage stepped to one side and turned. Past him, Tahiri saw the silvery-haired instructor climb up through what must have been a trapdoor that led up from beneath the hangar bay.

"I would rather not fight you," Tionne said. "But I will not allow you to hurt anyone in this room."

"Anakin," Tahiri whispered, "can Artoo help us?"

"Hah," Orloc said, pushing his purple cloak back from his shoulders. "What makes you think you can stop me?"

Ikrit clambered up out of the hole behind Tionne and crouched, watching the scene.

"The Force is with me," Tionne said. She swept a hand around to indicate Ikrit and the children. "The Force is with all of us."

"Well, Force or no Force, you don't look like much of a fighter," Orloc said. "I'll take my chances." He raised his glowing blade high in the air, ready to slice down on Tionne.

"Artoo, give me a high-frequency blast at full power," Anakin whispered.

Instantly a siren wail blared out of the little droid; the painfully loud alarm filled the entire hangar bay. The moment Orloc turned to look for the source of the sound, his lightsaber jumped from his grasp, flickered out, and floated away from him, high in the air over his head.

Before anyone realized what had happened, smoke spouted up from the place where Orloc stood, and when it cleared the Mage was gone.

"I wonder how he does that," Anakin said as the reunited companions gathered in the center of the hangar bay.

"I don't know, but at least he's gone," Tahiri said. She noticed that Ikrit—with Obi-Wan Kenobi's lightsaber in his furry paw—was carefully inspecting one of the ancient spaceships housed in the hangar bay.

"I'm not so sure," Uldir said. "By the way, thanks for coming to my rescue—all of you. You too, furball," he added, glancing at Ikrit.

"What do you mean you're not sure, Uldir?" Tionne asked.

"I mean I don't think he has gone yet," Uldir said. "He was looking for something called a holocr—Holocron. Yeah, that's it."

"There's a Holocron?" Tionne breathed. "Here? In Bast Castle? Where?"

"I think he said it was in some sort of room that Darth Vader used . . . his private quarters maybe."

Anakin and Tahiri looked at each other.

"Now *that's* interesting," Anakin said.

Tahiri grinned at Tionne. "If you really want to find that Holocron, I think Anakin and I can lead you to Vader's private quarters."

THIRTEEN

The glossy black walls and ceiling and floor of Darth Vader's personal chambers gleamed softly in the dim light. Uldir was impressed. It had been well over a decade since Darth Vader's death, and yet this room still felt like it belonged to a very powerful man. When Vader turned to the dark side, he had pledged himself to the Emperor's service—but look at all he had gotten in return! *Not a bad trade*, Uldir thought. Darth Vader's name had been known throughout the galaxy and he had enjoyed wealth and power for many years.

Darth Vader had chosen to be a powerful lord, not just an average Jedi. And best of all, Uldir mused, Vader had turned back to the light side at the end before he died, so that his family now remembered him with honor—and had even named a grandchild after him.

Anakin's voice broke into Uldir's thoughts. "Okay, I've got it."

The teenager turned and saw that Anakin was standing by a stone panel at the head of Darth Vader's sleeping cylinder. The slab looked just like all the other rock that lined the walls. When Anakin pushed on it, though, it slid silently to one side, revealing a small storage safe that opened at Anakin's voice command.

"Is it there?" Uldir asked. He thought of how exciting it would be to learn Jedi lessons about real power.

"Sure looks like it," Tahiri said. Artoo-Detoo burbled enthusiastically. Ikrit climbed onto Artoo-Detoo's domed head as Anakin withdrew the object from the safe.

"That's the Holocron all right," Tionne said. "It must be."

"Yes, an old one," Ikrit confirmed.

Anakin placed the glossy cube-shaped object into Tionne's hands, and Uldir moved closer. Her cheeks flushed and pink, the Jedi instructor looked at them with shining eyes. "This is a great treasure that belongs to all Jedi," she said. "It contains the teaching of a Jedi Master. Most Holocrons hold teachings of some sort, and some also contain songs, stories, legends. . . .

This is a great historical find. We'll take it to Master Skywalker at once." Tionne began leading them all toward the room's main entrance. "We can't let such an important treasure fall into the wrong hands or be used for one person's gain or glory."

"Does that mean we're leaving right now?" Anakin said.

"Uh-oh," groaned Tahiri. "More stairs."

Tionne smiled gratefully at Uldir. "Thank you very much for telling us the Holocron was here. I'm so excited I can hardly wait to see what it holds."

"Neither can I," said Uldir. "But how do we know it even works?"

The instructor's pearly eyes blinked with surprise. "I, well . . . I suppose we don't. I think it would be all right to test it." She sat on the floor and held her hands out in front of her, palms up. The others arranged themselves in a loose circle around the Holocron and sat down to watch. "Just a minute," Tionne said. The strange object rested lightly on her hands, as if floating on water.

A hologram blossomed in the air over the Holocron. "Welcome, my children. How may I teach you today? I am Asli Krimsan," said the glowing figure of a tiny plump woman with black hair and eyes the color of smoky topaz. She wore a long soft gown as red as wine. "I am a Jedi Master whose duty it has always been to teach those young ones who are gifted in the Force. Even before they become Jedi, the powerful ones must learn why they can sense people's feelings and how not to misuse that power. They must learn patience and Jedi relaxation techniques, and many other important things." The old woman's face shone with patient kindness. "Come listen to me, my child, and I will teach you."

Oh great. Baby lessons, Uldir thought. *Just what I need.* Well, he told himself, at least it looked as if the old lady would cover everything he might need to know to become a Jedi. And after all, he was pretty intelligent—how long could it take to learn it all?

"Let us begin with a Jedi relaxation technique. First I will show you how it looks on the outside; then I will describe how it feels inside."

Suddenly the hologram was hidden by a cloud of roiling gray smoke.

Uldir coughed. At first, he didn't understand what was happening.

Then he saw a flash of purple cloth and heard a gloating voice say, "Why, you didn't *really* think I would give up my prize so easily, did you?"

Uldir came to his feet, waving smoke away from his eyes. The Holocron was gone. "Neither will we, Orloc," he said.

"Then you'll have to catch me," the Mage countered.

Anakin looked around to see where Orloc might have gone with the Holocron. Ikrit or Tionne must have used the Force to clear the smoke away, he guessed, because within a second or two it was almost gone. The two Jedi opened the main chamber door and looked up and down the passageway. With a *whoosh,* the doors shut behind them, locking them out.

"He's in here!" Anakin shouted, pointing to the far end of the chamber behind the platform that held Darth Vader's sleeping cylinder. Orloc stood beside a control panel that had been hidden by a slab of polished black stone. Artoo-Detoo trilled a warning and moved to the door control panel by the main entrance, just behind Anakin.

"I'm coming," Tahiri called.

The Mage pressed a button—and Anakin jumped to safety a split second before a trapdoor opened in the floor where he had been standing. Artoo-Detoo tweedled frantically but was unable to close the pit in back of Anakin.

Anakin ran toward the Mage, who growled and pressed another button. Somewhere behind Anakin, Tahiri squealed. She must have jumped over a trapdoor, too, because the next sound

Anakin heard was the slap of her bare feet on the polished floor as she landed behind him.

Artoo-Detoo chittered angrily at the magician. Anakin kept running forward, with Tahiri following close after him.

The Mage merely chuckled and pushed a button to unseal a set of double doors behind him that led out of the chamber. They swung outward. Then, with one arm clutching the Holocron tightly to his chest, he reached out to push a final button on the control panel. A new trapdoor angled open between Anakin and the Mage, who stood in the doorway he had just unlocked.

Anakin stopped running and skidded to a halt right at the edge of the hole, with its steep, steep slide down into the secret depths of Bast Castle. Tahiri pulled him back before he could lose his balance and fall in. He gulped at the close call and glanced up to see a grin on Orloc's neatly bearded face, as if the magician were hoping they would fall down the chute.

The purple-robed Mage shrugged. "Too bad. Maybe some other day, hmmm?" He turned to leave. But Artoo-Detoo had managed to reverse the double doors from his control panel across the room. They were now swinging back toward Orloc. Soon there would be no place for the magician to stand as the doors swept backward toward the hole in the floor.

Beside Anakin, Tahiri gasped. The Mage tried

to push the doors forward, away from the edge of the pit. Anakin and Tahiri both stretched out their arms, trying to reach Orloc, but it was no use. As the doors shut he gave a yelp of alarm and flailed his arms in an attempt to keep his balance.

"Can you close the pit, Artoo?" Anakin called. Artoo buzzed twice.

Orloc threw his arms high into the air and let go of the precious Jedi cube, perhaps trying to grab on to something before he fell. The bobbled Holocron flew over Anakin's and Tahiri's heads as Orloc tumbled into the stone chute.

Dashing up behind them, Uldir caught the Holocron. "Got it!" he yelled. His voice cracked with triumph. At the door, Artoo finally succeeded in opening the main entrance again for Ikrit and Tionne. The two Jedi rushed back in.

With mixed feelings, Anakin looked down into the dark chute. He *should* have been able to do something more to keep Orloc from falling—but if they had managed to save him, wouldn't the Mage have tried to steal the Holocron from them again?

"Do you think he'll be all right?" Tahiri asked, looking down into the pit with a horrified expression on her face.

"Ikrit and I survived our fall," Tionne said softly from the other side of the room. "I think Orloc will be all right."

"Mmmm," Ikrit said. "I believe he is unhurt, that one."

"In fact," Tionne added with a dry note in her voice, "unless we get out of here soon, we probably haven't seen the last of him yet."

FOURTEEN

The unusual things they had seen and done since coming to Bast Castle amazed Anakin, but in the end there was one more surprise to come. Weary as the companions were, they were preparing to make the long climb back down to the *Lore Seeker* when Ikrit made a suggestion. "There is another way to get to your ship," he said.

Even before hearing his plan, Tahiri was enthusiastic.

Ikrit took them back to the hangar bay and showed them the ancient ships stored there. He had once owned just such a ship himself, and the controls could adjust to Ikrit's one-meter height. If the ships were kept in as good mechanical repair as everything else in Bast Castle seemed to be, it would take only a matter of minutes to fly down to the *Lore Seeker*. When a preflight check on their chosen ship showed that it was in excellent condition, everyone eagerly agreed to Ikrit's plan.

After Artoo-Detoo plugged into a control panel to open the hangar bay doors and make sure that all intruder defenses were turned off, they put Ikrit's plan into effect.

Ikrit did an expert job of piloting the old ship, and when they reached the *Lore Seeker* he seemed almost sad. Now it was Anakin's turn to make a surprising suggestion. "Why don't you keep the ship, Ikrit," he said. "It belonged to my grandfather, so I don't think there's anyone else who has a claim to it—and the controls are so old-fashioned that I'm not sure any other being would *want* it."

The Jedi Master seemed uncertain and looked hopefully at Tionne. A smile of delight spread across her face. "Of course—it would be just perfect for you." Anakin could have predicted that Tionne would like the idea, since she had such a love of history. Then Tionne frowned for a moment and looked over at Anakin. "But are you sure it's safe for him to fly it all the way back to Yavin 4?"

Anakin nodded. One of his special skills with the Force was knowing when machinery was working correctly, and he could sense that this ship was perfectly spaceworthy.

"It's in great shape," Uldir agreed. "I'll even be his copilot if you like. I've been a trained pilot for years, you know."

Tionne looked very pleased at this development. "Well, if it's all right with Ikrit, I guess it's all settled."

"You'll have to find a name for your ship by the time you get back to Yavin 4," Tahiri said, grinning. "I'll ask you about it."

To Anakin it seemed that Ikrit's white fur glowed with pride. "Mmmm," the Jedi Master said, nodding. "I will find a name for my ship."

A sea of green trees rippled below the *Lore Seeker* as it glided toward the landing field and the Jedi academy. For Anakin, the sight of the Great Temple standing in its clearing, drenched in bright sunlight, was a very welcome one indeed. "It feels good to be back," he said with a sigh.

Tahiri giggled. "That was certainly more of an adventure than I had bargained for."

Tionne looked at her two students. "Are you sorry you came with me?"

Anakin shook his head. "The trip was worth making. I learned some interesting things about Darth Vader."

"I learned to trust the Force and not just my eyes and ears," Tahiri said.

"And we did find a lightsaber and a Holocron," Anakin said.

"And a new ship for Ikrit," Tahiri added. "So I think we're glad we came along, but it may be a while before we go looking for adventures again."

Tionne brought the *Lore Seeker* down on the landing field, where Luke Skywalker was waiting for them. As soon as she opened the exit hatch, Anakin and Tahiri tumbled out of the ship, anxious to greet Luke and share their news with him.

"We've got some surprises for you, Uncle Luke," Anakin said.

"Just wait until you see what we've found," Tahiri said. "You'll never believe it." Her green eyes danced with excitement. "We'll have to let Tionne tell you the biggest news, though."

Tionne came out of the *Lore Seeker* then, followed by Artoo-Detoo, who burbled a happy greeting.

"It's good to have you back, Artoo," Luke said. "From all the excitement, I take it you found the lightsaber."

"And more," Tionne answered, holding out the Holocron for him to see. "Master Ikrit has the lightsaber with him."

"But where *are* Uldir and Ikrit?" Luke asked, looking at the new Holocron with wonder.

"There," said Tionne, pointing to a speck above the treetops with a proud smile.

"We found a new ship, and Ikrit's flying it," Anakin explained.

"A really *old* ship, actually," Tahiri put in.

Luke's eyebrows went up. "That certainly is interesting news," he said. He watched with fascination while the ancient ship landed a short way from the *Lore Seeker* and Ikrit and Uldir got out.

"Welcome back," Luke said. "Let's all go inside where you can rest and share your news with me."

"What did you name the ship?" Tahiri asked Ikrit as they walked back toward the Great Temple.

"It's a good name," Uldir said, but he seemed distracted. The teenager stopped and looked up at the sky, as if still thinking about their adventure and the strange Mage they had met.

"I have named her the *Sunrider,*" said Ikrit.

"After Nomi Sunrider?" Tionne asked with a delighted smile.

"Yes, the Jedi Master who lived long ago," Ikrit said.

Everyone approved of the name. When they reached the base of the Great Temple, Luke started to climb the steps that ran up one of its four sides. Tahiri groaned and stood as still as if her bare feet were rooted to the ground.

"Um, Uncle Luke," Anakin said, "would you mind very much if we went in through the hangar bay and took the turbolift?"

Luke raised his eyebrows at the unusual request.

Tahiri giggled. "I think we've all had enough stairs in the past few days to last us a long, long time," she said.

STAR WARS

Junior Jedi Knights

Kenobi's Blade

Uldir, Anakin's classmate at the Jedi academy, wants to be a Jedi more than anything. But he can't even lift a feather with the Force. He thinks he knows how he can learn faster: the Holocron.

The Holocron is a cube that holds all the secrets of the ancient Jedi Masters. By "borrowing" it, along with Obi-Wan Kenobi's lightsaber, Uldir believes he will become a powerful Jedi Knight!

Now Anakin—along with Tahiri, R2-D2, Tionne and the Jedi Master Ikrit—must race across the galaxy to find Uldir. If they don't, Uldir could be killed. And Kenobi's blade and the Holocron will fall into the hands of a very evil man . . .

Turn the page for a special preview of the next book in the STAR WARS: JUNIOR JEDI KNIGHTS series: KENOBI'S BLADE.

Tahiri loved the feel of the Great Temple's smooth, cool stones beneath her bare feet. She hummed a soft tune under her breath while she walked up and down the halls, but her mind was set on just one thing: finding Uldir. The teenager was already more than an hour late for a practice session he and Tahiri had planned this morning. It wasn't like her friend to be late.

Anakin had gone for an early walk in the jungle with Master Ikrit. They wouldn't be back until time for the midmorning lesson, so Tahiri decided to look for Uldir alone. She started with the kitchens. When she stuck her head in to look around, the food-prep area was bustling with activity. The scents of baking bread, stewing meats and vegetables, and freshly sliced fruits filled the air. Half a dozen cooks, servers, and cleaning people scurried about doing their chores, but Tahiri saw no sign of Uldir's shaggy chestnut hair or broad shoulders. In fact, the kitchen staff said that Uldir had not been in all morning.

Tahiri shook her head and yanked thoughtfully at a strand of blond hair. This was not like Uldir *at all*.

Next she tried the Grand Audience Chamber, where Uldir sometimes went to think. But this morning the huge auditorium stood completely empty. Tahiri looked in every one of Uldir's favorite places, both inside the Great Temple and out. She even searched on the landing field and noticed that Ikrit's ship, the *Sunrider,* was gone. The white-furred Jedi Master must have changed his mind and taken Anakin for a short flight instead of a walk, she guessed.

Tahiri headed back inside. She was beginning to get worried about her friend. After checking the docking bay, the rear steps of the temple, and the comm center, her worry turned to alarm. Then, like a blaster bolt, it struck her—she hadn't actually *looked* inside his room! She had only knocked once, and given up when there had been no reply.

Of course, if Uldir *was* still in his room and hadn't answered her knock, that probably meant he was sick or upset over something. Still, she was relieved. She began humming her little tune again as she

114

hurried toward his quarters as fast as her bare feet could carry her. At the door to her friend's room, Tahiri raised a small, strong hand and rapped sharply on the thick wood.

"Uldir, it's me," she sang out. "Can I talk to you?" When there was no reply, she tried again. "Uldir, are you all right? May I come in?" Again, no answer.

Tahiri sensed nothing from behind the door. Nothing at all. What if her friend was really sick or unconscious? She would have to look. Carefully she eased the door open a crack and peeked in. The sleeping pallet in the corner was empty.

Pushing the door open so that she could step inside, Tahiri called, "Uldir?" The room was empty. Completely empty. Not a trace of her friend. She even checked the refresher unit, but the door stood open and the cubicle was empty.

Something was very wrong here.

A feeling of dread clamped itself around Tahiri's chest, making it hard for her to breathe. In the little trunk where Uldir kept his few possessions, Tahiri found nothing. She whirled and looked at the wall. No flight suit or Jedi robes dangled from the pegs there. Uldir was *gone*.

But where?

Anakin always enjoyed walks with Ikrit. Now that they were back, the white-furred Jedi Master sat on the windowsill sunning himself while Anakin got ready for his morning lesson. Artoo-Detoo stood in the corner nearby; the little droid always stayed close to Anakin when Master Skywalker was gone. Anakin had just finished pulling on a fresh flight suit when Tahiri burst into the room.

Pale yellow hair damp with sweat clung to her forehead. Her emerald green eyes blazed like they always did when she had something important to tell him.

"Uldir's not here!" Tahiri blurted out. "I can't find him anywhere. I looked all over the Great Temple while you and Master Ikrit were flying around in the *Sunrider*. No one has seen him all morning, and his room is empty. Well, aren't you going to say anything?" She rushed on before Anakin could grasp what she was telling him. "Even his clothes were gone, and his blanket. Everything. There's nothing at—"

"Wait a minute," Anakin said, trying hard to let his mind catch up with Tahiri's words. "Who told you that Master Ikrit and I were in the *Sunrider*? We went for a walk this morning."

"Well, one of the places I looked for Uldir was on the landing field, and when I noticed that the *Sunrider* was gone, I naturally figured that you and Master Ikrit were . . ." Her words trailed off.

Anakin shook his head.

Ikrit spoke up from the windowsill. "Mmmmmm, the girl is right. My ship no longer stands on the landing field." Artoo-Detoo gave an astonished-sounding twitter.

"I've got a strange feeling about this," Anakin said.

Just then, their teacher Tionne appeared in the doorway. A worried frown drew her silvery brows together and creased her forehead. When she saw her two students with the Jedi Master, her face cleared.

"Oh, *there* you are. Did you borrow the Holocron, Master Ikrit? I wanted to ask it something before our morning lesson. But when I went to get it from Master Skywalker's room, the table where I had put it and Obi-Wan Kenobi's lightsaber was empty."

Anakin had been with Ikrit all morning and knew that the Jedi Master did not have the Holocron. When Anakin saw Ikrit's fluffy white ears droop, a dozen pieces of puzzle fell into place in his mind.

"I'm afraid I know where the Holocron is," Anakin said heavily. "And Obi-Wan Kenobi's lightsaber, too. I think they're in the *Sunrider.*" He glanced up at Tahiri and watched his friend's green eyes go wide with shock as she realized what he meant.

His teacher Tionne, however, looked confused. "Why? Who put them in Master Ikrit's ship?"

Ikrit sprang down from the windowsill. "We must go after the boy," the white-furred Jedi said, as if the question had already been answered. "The Holocron is valuable. Although only a Jedi can use it, the boy could be in more danger than he suspects."

"Who?" Tionne asked again. "Why is the Holocron in the *Sunrider?*"

Anakin looked at the Jedi teacher. "Uldir is gone," he said. "Tahiri looked and his rooms are empty."

"No one has seen him since last night," Tahiri put in.

"The *Sunrider* is also missing," Ikrit added.

Tionne closed her mother-of-pearl eyes and nodded her understanding. "And now the Holocron and Obi-Wan Kenobi's lightsaber are missing, too. I see." She opened her eyes again, and her face held a look of determination. "You're right, Master Ikrit. We'll have to go after Uldir. There's no time to lose." She glanced back at Anakin.

"I think I know where Uldir might be heading." Anakin brushed the fringe of dark hair away from his eyes. Another piece of the puzzle had just clicked into place. "Exis," he said. "The space station. He probably thinks that's the best place to learn to be a Jedi."

"And he said that Mage Orloc talked about Exis Station, too," Tahiri reminded him.

"Can you fly us to Exis in the *Lore Seeker?*" Ikrit asked Tionne.

"Yes," Tionne said. "I remember how to get there. I can program the coordinates into the *Lore Seeker*'s navigational computers."

Artoo-Detoo warbled and bleeped.

"Of *course* we'll take you along as our navigator, Artoo," Anakin said.

"I'm sure Master Skywalker would approve," Tionne agreed.

"What if Uldir just left for a little while? Maybe he'll come back by himself," Tahiri suggested.

"All right. Gather everything you'll need for our trip," Tionne answered. "I'll have the Great Temple searched again. But if the *Sunrider* and Uldir aren't here by this evening, we leave for Exis Station."

Alone at the controls of the ship, Uldir reached up and flipped a few switches overhead. The *Sunrider* shuddered and dropped out of hyperspace at the edge of the Teedio System.

Uldir gave a whoop of triumph. He had made it. He was almost there. For a few minutes at the beginning of his trip, Uldir had wondered if he would truly be able to navigate and pilot the *Sunrider* all by himself, but he was a good pilot and he had succeeded. Uldir knew from what Asli Krimsan and Tionne had said that the space station was a safe distance from the sun, somewhere in the Teedio System. The coordinates for the system had been easy to find in the *Sunrider*'s navicomputer. Now that he had arrived, he'd have to scan for the station itself, but something that large, he figured, should be simple enough to locate.

"Way to go, hotshot," he congratulated himself, proud of a job well done. "I'll bet you could fly just about *any* ship if you had to." His parents, who were shuttle pilots for the New Republic, had taught him well.

He checked his coordinates and began a survey of the Teedio System, searching for Exis Station. Within minutes a blip appeared on the control panel in front of him. The thing was too big to be another ship, Uldir decided. The blip was the right size, shape, and age, and it was just about where Tionne said she had left the space station.

Uldir grinned and laid in a new course straight to the station. The distant stars seemed to hold a welcoming twinkle, and Uldir told himself that he was definitely doing the right thing.

Or was he?

Flying the *Sunrider* alone had been such a challenge that Uldir had not let himself think about what he had done up to this point. Now that he was finally close to his destination, though, doubts crept into his mind. Had the dark side of the Force brought him here? After all, he had stolen the ship and the Holocron and the lightsaber—no, he had *borrowed* them, Uldir corrected himself.

A new thought sent a jolt of fear through him. What if Orloc no longer lived at Exis? Or what if he did, but refused to help Uldir? Uldir set his mouth in a grim line. Well then, he would just stay at the space station without the Mage and study until he became a Jedi.

Perhaps in this place that had once held a great library of the Jedi, the Holocron would work for Uldir. He would learn its secrets and return to his friends a full-fledged Jedi. He would show them that he could make something of himself. But what if he *was* just falling to the dark side of the Force by coming here? Uldir snorted. Sometimes a Jedi had to make difficult decisions, he assured himself.

What choices did he have left, after all? Master Skywalker had said he saw no Jedi potential in Uldir. And outside the cave on Dathomir, the furball Ikrit had said there was nothing there for Uldir, for whom the cave had seemed empty. Tahiri and Anakin had claimed to have strange experiences in the cave, and Uldir now believed them. What Uldir did *not* believe was that these "failures" meant he could never become a Jedi. They simply meant that traditional teaching didn't work for him. Well, he had seen another chance and he had taken it. He'd soon find out if the risk had been worth it. He allowed himself a small smile. At least this time he wasn't a stowaway.

Uldir sat up straighter in the pilot's seat as he caught his first good glimpse of Exis. It looked like a many-armed sea creature made of metal, turning slowly in space. It was much larger than he had expected. The center of the space station was shaped like a thick, solid wheel. Satellite stations of all shapes and sizes were connected to the central hub by wide access tubes. He couldn't tell what the smaller stations were for, but he would ignore them, he decided, and head straight for the hub.

Now came one of the trickier parts of his plan. He couldn't be sure whether anyone was there on the space station monitoring the docking bays. However, most space stations had at least one fully automated emergency dock for use only by captains of damaged ships or travelers who were injured or ill.

Taking a deep breath and holding it, Uldir sent the age-old signal that identified him as a ship in distress. For a long moment nothing happened. Uldir's stomach churned, and still he held his breath. He gritted his teeth. What if he had guessed wrong? What if he had come all this way and there was no way to get aboard Exis Station?

Suddenly an opening appeared in the side of the space station as a wide bay door slid aside. Rippling rows of bright lights appeared in the hangar bay walls to guide Uldir's ship into position. Letting out his breath, Uldir took the *Sunrider* in for a landing.

Except for the usual clanks, hums, buzzes, and thumps made by a working space station, Uldir was greeted by silence when he stepped out into the sealed hangar bay. There was plenty of breathable air in the station—he had checked before leaving the ship.

Uldir clipped Obi-Wan Kenobi's lightsaber to the belt he wore around his Jedi robe. He stuffed the Holocron into a full supply satchel and slung the strap over his shoulder. He looked around and snorted.

"Not much of a welcoming committee," he muttered. Then he remembered that emergency docks were normally sealed off from the rest of the space station, in case the "emergency" happened to be a transport filled with spies or a ship about to explode. Even if Orloc was somewhere on Exis, he probably didn't know of Uldir's arrival.

It was dark inside—not as dark as space itself, but dark enough to make Uldir shiver. Once the hangar bay doors had automatically shut, the lights had dimmed again, so Uldir rummaged through his satchel and pulled out a glowrod. Turning it to its brightest setting, he raised the light high and looked around.

Exis Station's emergency hangar bay was enormous, able to hold much larger ships than Ikrit's little *Sunrider*. The light from the glowrod didn't even reach the ceiling. Shadows sucked away at the edges of his light.

"Spooky old place," Uldir mumbled. He jumped at the sudden hissing and ticking sound that came from behind him, but it was only the *Sunrider*'s engines cooling. He laughed at himself. He hadn't realized how tense this new situation had made him.

Holding the glowrod with shaking fingers, he headed toward the back of the docking bay until his light fell on a sealed air-lock door. Uldir walked the length of the wall once, but the air-lock door was the only exit. Sealed with blast-shielding, the door was only large enough to accommodate one person at a time—probably as a security precaution. Any intruders who tried to attack the space station from this emergency hangar bay would have to do so one by one.

Not knowing what to expect, Uldir reached for the air-lock control switch. To his surprise, it slid open at his touch. It was unlocked and required no access code.

Uldir stepped into the air lock with a smile of satisfaction and let it slide shut. Next he threw the switch for the second door. When the door slid open, his mouth fell open too.

Waiting for him on the other side was one of the strangest sights Uldir had ever seen.

About a dozen droids of every shape and description stood, sat, trundled, or hovered in a rough semicircle outside the air lock. In front of the droids crouched a handful of large rodentlike creatures with gray-brown fur. The creatures, who wore purple sashes around their waists and silver armbands, would have been about as tall as his shoulder had they been standing. Uldir knew what they were, for he had seen some once on Tatooine: they were Ranats.

And each of them was holding a blaster—pointed straight at him.

He froze. Before Uldir could even speak, someone or something threw a rough sack over his head and pushed him to the floor. Tiny fingers with sharp claws tied his hands and feet together.

Uldir thought of calling for help, but he knew there was no one to call to. When he tried to speak, he felt a sharp sting, as if a needle had pricked his arm. Then came a fizzy feeling, like he sometimes had when his foot feel asleep . . . only this was all over his body. Then the darkness inside the sack turned even darker, and Uldir passed out.

Uldir didn't know how long he was unconscious, but when he woke up he found himself on something hard and flat that was moving. Probably a stretcher or a repulsorsled, he guessed. He heard the voices of the Ranats chittering around him. They were not speaking Basic, so he couldn't understand what they were saying.

The sled hummed and rocked softly as they moved along. Minutes crept by and became half an hour, then an hour. Uldir stopped trying to keep track of the time. His arms and legs still had the fizzy feeling. Perhaps this time they were truly asleep.

At last, after what might have been hours, the Ranats and the clanking droids and the repulsorsled came to a stop. The platform Uldir lay on stopped humming, as if someone had flicked a switch, and he fell half a meter to land painfully on the floor. He struggled back up into a sitting position. Someone yanked the sack off his head.

Uldir blinked in the sudden brightness of a clean, well-lit room. The walls and floors were of polished metal, and plush cushions lay scattered on the deck plates.

Suddenly a plume of smoke billowed up from amongst the cushions and Uldir heard a voice say, "Why, I do believe we have a visitor."

When the smoke cleared, Uldir saw a thin man wearing a deep purple cloak with silver spangles along its edges. The man threw back the hood of his cloak to reveal long dark hair, tawny eyes, and a small, neat beard. But Uldir already knew who he was.

It was the Mage Orloc.

ABOUT THE AUTHOR

REBECCA MOESTA ANDERSON has known shc wanted to be an author since her early teens, but it wasn't until six years ago that she began writing in earnest. Rebecca has worked on numerous *Star Wars* projects. With her husband, KEVIN J. ANDERSON, she created and wrote the young adult novels in the YOUNG JEDI KNIGHTS series and two high-tech pop-up books. She has also authored several science fiction stories (both on her own and with her husband) and has cowritten three science fiction and fantasy novels under a pseudonym.

Born in Heidelberg, Germany, to American parents, Rebecca was raised in Pasadena, California. After receiving a Master's of Science degree in Business Administration from Boston University, she worked for more than seven years as a technical editor and writer at Lawrence Livermore National Laboratory, a large government research facility in California.

Rebecca Moesta has one son, who keeps her busy nearly every minute that she doesn't spend writing.

Rebecca Moesta and Kevin J. Anderson's
WordFire website may be reached at
http://www.wordfire.com